7.13
Brooklyn, NY

ADVANCE PRAISE

"Alex Behr's imagination is wild, rigorous, and totally unique. I haven't been able to decide if her stories are comedies intercut with horror or horror stories leavened by comedy, but when they're this entertaining, who cares?"
— Tom Bissell, author of *Apostle: Travels Among the Tombs of the Twelve*

"Alex Behr's *Planet Grim* turned me inside out. No, really, these stories of eros and ids getting loose, inner contradictions and desires crashing into each other like marbles, brutal instances of violence up against a moment of tender beauty, the people and lovers and mothers and families in this book are carved from the guts of us. What sits dead center at this hybrid of self and other is, mercifully, an unbeaten heart."
— Lidia Yuknavitch, author of *The Book of Joan* and *The Small Backs of Children*

"Alex Behr's characters are conflicted, uncertain, and pained. What's so compelling about her fiction is how she honors that conflictedness, explores the uncertainties, and examines the pain until it reveals itself as irreducibly human and therefore a kind of grace."
— Dan DeWeese, author of *You Don't Love This Man* and *Disorder*

"In Alex Behr's funny, poignant stories, the kids are sharp, fearless, and insatiable, the parents conflicted, lustful, and tough. The meaning of family and love is an epic game nobody can win or stop playing."
— Mary Rechner, author of the story collection *Nine Simple Patterns for Complicated Women*

Printed and distributed by 7.13 Books. First paperback edition, first printing: October 2017

Cover design: Gigi Little
Cover photo: Lewis Watts
Author photo: Heather Maxwell Hall

ISBN-10: 0-9984092-2-7
ISBN-13: 978-0-9984092-2-1

Library of Congress Control Number: 2017944227

This collection is available in a variety of electronic formats including EPUB for mobile devices, MOBI for Kindles, and PDFs for American and European laser printers.

www.713books.com

For Eli Zheng
We vibrate in space

Lent
Conseillez-vous soigneusement
Munissez-vous de clairvoyance
Seul, pendant un instant
De manière à obtenir un creux
Très perdu
Portez cela plus loin
Ouvrez la tête
Enfouissez le son

—Erik Satie

Slow. Advise yourself carefully. Arm yourself with clairvoyance. Alone for an instant. So that you obtain a hollow. Very lost. Carry that further. Open your head. Bury the sound. Gnoissienne no. 3 (1890).

Contents

WHITE PANTS

I'm envious of anyone who can wear white pants. I'm much too broad and slovenly. That's not to say I didn't give them a chance. In sixth grade, we liked wearing cotton painters pants, the ones with the hammer loops and tool pockets. We accessorized them with cowl neck shirts and heavy clogs. I don't know why that look became popular—maybe in the hopes a boy would stick his hand in a loop and pull you toward him? And if you didn't like him, you could stomp him like an angry horse?

One day in April, I stood with my class in the school auditorium. Our school was in southeast Portland, near Mount Tabor. I swung a hand bell and sang the lyrics to "Oregon, My Oregon." On portable bleachers, everyone sounded pure and clean. None of the boys' voices had changed yet, but we were devious monsters. I kept a long comb in my side pocket, but didn't want to use it afterward, for fear of finding someone's spitball.

Menstrual cramps pinched the sides of my stomach, and Bobby's body odor made me woozy. I stared at the clock, wishing it would get a shot of adrenaline and push the day to its conclusion. Bobby stood next to me, and I inched to the edge of the bleacher, one clog half covering the other. Bobby wore the same sweatshirt most days, blue with the wristbands cut off. He rarely bathed.

Every school had at least one stinky kid. Some you might not guess were stinky until they banged you into a locker, but this kid had a sour milk smell like a devil swirl. It was the stink of being poor. I had that prejudice then, but now I know better. It was probably just some soap I didn't like. I was so arrogant.

My name is Tara, but Bobby said "Tata," right in my ear. It didn't matter that kids were singing. I could hear it over the xylophones in front and patriotic songs all around. His words could be any volume, and I'd hear that name.

Onstage, my Love's Baby Soft deodorant mixed with tangy menstrual blood. Or so I feared. My nose played tricks on me. I believed I could feel the blood seeping through the double-stitched seam of my white pants. Truly a curse, to be a "woman" so young, not even twelve. We had only one song to go. Hoping the stain wouldn't spread, I held my song folder over my crotch.

I talked to God, pleading. I stared into the red and green stage lights, as if punishing my retinas would get God's notice and have Him reactivate the magma beneath Mount Tabor. I could run offstage, but the fifth graders waited in the wings, making farting noises into their elbows.

Bobby stared at me, not bothering to sing. He put

his bell down and pulled off his sweatshirt. "Take it," he said, as if we were about to snowball at the ice rink. "I don't need it." I shook my head, my leg rattling the bleacher. Brenda and Vanessa turned around to look at me, wide-eyed, as if I didn't remember they had lice in fourth grade and had to have their hair chopped off.

A kindergartner in a green jumper sat cross-legged on the floor and pointed at me. I had noticed her earlier. She picked a scab from her knee and ate it. She would learn shame soon enough. Maybe she knew shame already, but not this female loathing. I dropped my hand bell to the stage, as if by accident, and jumped down, landing on my knees with my rear sticking up. The music teacher tapped her stick on the lectern. The kids on the bleachers clapped with her, as if she were doing a rhythm exercise. She had hairy arms so we called her a lezzy. She hated us. "Tara," she said, interrupting the music. "This isn't an acrobatics class." She pointed to the bleachers and ordered me to finish the program.

I crouched with my turquoise shirt pulled over my knees, wondering whether to skitter across the stage like a rabid fox. The kids on the bleachers kept clapping. I felt something on my shoulders. Bobby had dropped his sweatshirt on me.

It must have been his dad's or his older brother's. It smelled like cigarettes. I put it on and it fell to my thighs. I hobbled to the side of the stage, past the fifth graders and my old teacher, who looked at me with pity.

I went to the school nurse and had her call my

mom. Bobby, in trouble again, sat next to me in the secretary's office. I took the sweatshirt off and handed it to him. Kids might see us when they walked past the open door, and I didn't want anyone to think we were dating. I found my social equal, and he had a wart on the fleshy part by his thumb.

"I like you, Tata," he said. "You're OK." The secretary ripped the page out of the typewriter and told us to be quiet. She had a shag and wore long feather earrings, which I coveted. I knew she felt sorry for me, because she gave me a corduroy skirt to put on from the lost-and-found box. She said she couldn't reach my mom, so I could wear the skirt.

I pushed Bobby's arm away and told him not to touch me. But I know this now: Bobby was the first of many guys who found me pathetic, who saw me as a project.

I didn't think of him for years, because he moved away—his new stepdad was in the Air Force and got stationed in Mountain Home, Idaho. He sent me a letter, though. He sent me a bunch, which got progressively stranger, even though his spelling improved. He told me he wanted to take out my eyes, which are green, and put them in a jar by his bed. He meant it as a compliment.

In tenth grade, I started cutting school. My mom had left us for a boyfriend in California, so I had to help my dad at his store. I didn't feel sorry for myself, because my mom was barely there to begin with. Well, I hated her at first, but what good did that do? She couldn't feel it from such a distance. She sent me fortune cookie messages, which I pasted on the slats of my bed. I didn't want my dad to read them.

One afternoon, I saw a crow's head on the sidewalk. I thought it was part of an electric shoe brusher, like my grandpa had in his bathroom: red bristles on one side and black on the other. I couldn't figure out why the brush would be left outside. Then I noticed the beak, curved, ready to pierce. The head lay on the damp pavement, by rock walls sprouting moss and ferns and a rhododendron thick with buds.

This crow's head didn't get a proper burial, because its body and wings were missing. I ripped notebook paper from a binder and picked up the head, making sure I didn't see any maggots. I put it in my backpack and crossed matted leaves from the storm the day before. The leaves, twigs, and mud covered the sidewalk as if reclaiming a piece of the forest understory. Slabs of rocks stood upright in front yards like nameless graves.

On the way to my boyfriend Ebin's house, the sidewalk was stained brown from crushed leaves. I passed a billboard in a fenced-in yard, with only a couple of PBR cans for company. It used to advertise Virginia Slims cigarettes, but now the peeling layers looked like an eviscerated patchwork quilt.

Outside Ebin's house, the lower halves of the trees were painted white with red diamonds. Beside the trunks, Ebin had nailed dominoes around a telephone pole, like a strange Morse code. Portland tolerated eccentrics. Plastic trolls, Barbie dolls, and a horseshoe surrounded a red fuse box nailed in the center. He'd written on its door, "Only the pure of heart may enter." I opened the box, but it was empty. I put the crow's head inside. I had seen Ebin with another girl; I found a note from her in the vest I'd lent him. I had lent him almost all my savings so he could get his cab license, and he screwed me over. I walked away from the box, hoping no one saw me.

I skipped the last class to help out my dad. He needed to keep his junk shop going, if only to keep his mind off my mom, and he couldn't afford a real worker. To lure in customers, my dad had put a Holy Qur'an in the front case by the dime store paperback *Lady, That's My Skull.* He thought he would meet someone who could explain the synchronicity between the books, but so far, no one had. Inside, I greeted the lawn ornament, a boy holding a lantern. My mom, before she left, wrote a sign for him: THIS STORE IS FULL OF OLD, FRAGILE, SHARP, AND UNCLEANED CURIOUS GOODS. BUYERS BEWARE. I interpreted her words as a message to me, that I was fragile, and I dreamed of heading south to San Francisco. If it was good enough for my mom, it was good enough for me. At least I would be free of Ebin.

From the rafters hung dolls and coats—some from Goodwill and some from customers careless enough to leave them behind. No longer in white pants, I wore black most of the time, like a cutoff flannel nightgown, dyed with RIT in the sink. I turned on a Kurosawa video to watch on the TV behind the counter.

Outside, a city worker used a concrete saw to access the sewer main. Throughout Portland, people obsessed about water—either what fell most of the year or what poured into the river in barely filtered pipes. That's why I dreamt of San Francisco: for its concrete and fog. The low, grinding sound filled the store. The grunting samurai on the TV screen could not compete, so I put it on mute.

I ripped out photos from an album that we'd gotten from an estate sale. They dropped into a barrel for sale at fifty cents each. I fell in love with the family whose history I disassembled, like a jigsaw puzzle in reverse. The birth announcement in the front of the album said they lived in Aloha, Oregon. Their boy, Martin, posed in Marlboro and whiskey boxes or crouched by a bunny. Martin aged in the photos, often holding toy guns, first pointed at the anonymous photographer, and now at me.

I didn't like friends visiting the store, much less Ebin. I didn't want them to think my dad was a pervert, instead of a smart businessman. Randy, my dad, sold stacks of photos from the 1960s of women who had hoped to get into *Playboy.* Answering ads at the back of dirty magazines, the women or their boyfriends sent in nudie pictures with the models' anxious smiles, bangs, boobs, ass, and the rest all displayed on vinyl lawn chairs, or on beds with chenille bedspreads, maybe teddy bears behind them.

One time Ebin had found a pamphlet for a Canadian nudist colony; the cover showed a fir tree with the picnic table blocking the father's dick and the daughter—maybe twelve years old—looking as if the tree trunk was growing out of her head. I'd read enough Freud to be both disgusted and amused. The girl folded her legs and arms up to be modest, though I wondered about that—wasn't the point of a nudist colony to have no shame? I didn't like the thought of all this porn around my dad; it was gross. But he said this soft stuff sold well to collectors. Ebin took the pamphlet, as if dating me meant a stake in the store.

The sewer workers finally stopped, and the doorbell rang. I dipped my hand into a bag of Cheetos, wiping orange dust across my lips. My dad's friend Tim came in holding a cardboard box. "Is your dad here?" he asked.

I preferred not to answer him, but he wouldn't give up. "He's at the bank," I said. "Come back at five."

He put the box on a stool, leaned on the counter, and pointed to a stack of postcards under glass. "Can you get those out, ma'am?" he asked.

The cards were taken in World War II. I couldn't stand them. "You look at them yourself," I said. I went back to the photo album from Aloha, with the family posing at Cannon Beach. The grandma in her dark overcoat dwarfed the little boy. Once again, he held a toy gun in his hand. The muzzle faced me.

"How do you like this one?" Tim asked. He held up a postcard of beaten American soldiers in a Japanese prison camp. One man wore a black scarf around his eyes, as if he were facing execution.

"Put them away, please," I said. I wished I had a

cigarette to blow smoke in his face. He hated the smell.

He took a Cheeto from my bag and put the box on the counter. I gave in to curiosity and looked inside. I saw a pieces of bone, dusty bowls, and spear points.

Tim slapped the postcards down. "This stuff I got is authentic. I've got people working for me. You wouldn't want to know them. Let's just say they're better my friends than yours. But that doesn't mean I can't be your friend." He placed a paperback on the counter—*Hong Kong Madam*. "Put that toward my credit."

I ignored him. I tore out a picture of Martin sitting on Santa's lap. He held his fingers together in the shape of a diamond, under silvery decorations.

"These are valuable artifacts," he said. He picked up a bone from the box and handed it to me. "It's a real kneecap. Think about it. Those Indians worshipped this shit. It's dug up from a grave in the desert. Someone went to the trouble of burying this poor fool hundreds of years ago, not knowing it'd turn a profit someday."

I traced the edge of the kneecap and glanced at my own, behind the counter.

Then Randy came into the store and Tim greeted him. He was taller than Tim, taller than most people, and wore a suit and a bowler hat from the 1940s. He had a long moustache that he greased into points. He tried to look eccentric so people wouldn't think he was smart. It helped him make better deals.

Randy pointed to the pile on the counter. "That can't stay here," he said to Tim. "Let's take it in the back and see what you have." He winked and handed me a ten-dollar bill. "Keep the change."

I slammed the door as I left, disgusted. I had Martin's photo with Santa. It had their address on the back. I contemplated going out to Aloha. His childhood house had a clothesline out back and fields of corn. But Martin was an adult now, and that store Santa was probably dead.

I went back to Ebin's neighborhood. The crow head was still inside the fuse box. I gingerly removed it, holding my breath. It started to rain. I tossed the head under a bush. I put the photo from Martin's album in the box instead, next to a child's birthday candle shaped like a clown. I wrote on the back of the photo for Ebin to call me. Remember, these boy-men believed they could save me, and part of their pity made them come back, eventually.

Ebin and I moved to San Francisco, ending up in a rehabbed school bus, out in China Basin. I had to leave—my dad started selling more stolen relics and I had to either call him in or call in his friend—I chose Tim and I was afraid. I never told anyone, but now he's stuck in jail. I didn't have to testify because the detectives found boxes of shit he'd stolen at his storage unit. It turned out that Tim had speed freaks to work for him. They got loaded and worked for hours, combing the desert. A couple even smashed dusty museum cases up the Columbia River.

I gained weight from lack of exercise and a diet of store-bought food. Maybe I was scared, too, that

Tim or his friends would find me. I wanted padding, psychologically. We cooked on a hot plate because we parked by a building with an electrical outlet on the outside. We could even watch TV. The cops bothered us only on street cleaning days. China Basin in those days was empty, just gulls and stray dogs and us.

One day, I bought a pair of white pants from a guy in the Mission. I wasn't worried about getting them bloody, like in sixth grade. I had stopped menstruating, because I was on the pill. When you lived in a bus, you didn't want to mess with tampons, and I certainly didn't want to get pregnant. The guy had a sidewalk sale set up in front of a movie theater that showed Fellini and the usual art crap. The rest of his junk looked pilfered—brass candlesticks, paperbacks, votive candles, a My Little Pony with its tail ripped out.

I held up the white pants in front of me, judging that they'd fit. They had rhinestones down the sides. I ducked into a bookstore to put them on. It was next to the café where the Mission's Red Man sat all day, his face covered with a thin sheen of red face paint.

I put on the pants, forcing up the zipper, and followed a girl who also wore white pants. I followed people for sport, not loneliness. She had bleached white hair, like Debbie Harry, and wore high heels with a white blouse and white pants. All that white blinded me. I felt like I'd met my twin, only someone with more sex trapped in fabric and leather shoes. I crossed in front of blatting scooters and cars, not pausing, knowing the vehicles measured their speed based on mine, and I was matching hers.

I followed her as far as a tamales cart and I let her go. She was looking back at me, and I had nothing to say.

I knew when I married Ebin that it was stupid. He proposed to me with a ring from one of those dollar stores on 24th and Mission. He sang me an Elvis song, and it was so off-key I gave in and said yes. Besides, my dad and my close friends thought it was a terrible idea, which was a great incentive to disregard their advice. We even bought a piñata to celebrate and filled it with trinkets and fortune cookies from our favorite Chinese place.

He collected underground comics and put blankets over the bus windows, so he could read in the dark all day. He stopped washing his socks, buying new ones with a poor person's mentality. He shopped at the cheap stores on Mission, which either got them from outlets or stolen off a truck or something. They usually held up around five washes or so. He didn't think to invest in good pairs.

He had a talent, but he wasted it at first. He drew on things all the time: Styrofoam cups, Post-Its, sneakers, MUNI buses, abandoned brick buildings, and, of course, highway underpasses in the Mission, close to his favorite bars. He used Sharpies and spray paint, which gave the bus a chemical smell, but I didn't mind.

He used to draw all over my skin, but that stopped after we got married. He stayed skinny and I got fat, like the nursery rhyme about Jack Sprat and his unnamed wife. We licked the platter clean, until there was nothing left to enjoy.

Ebin, before he got famous, made triangle origami dogs. Just four folds—one for the head, two for the ears, and one for the bottom of the head. We scattered them on the floor of the bus, with our dirty socks and doll heads. We didn't care. I thought Life would care; that God, a facet of Life, didn't like clutter and would judge us, but the more cluttered the bus became the less I cared. Since we were made in His image, I couldn't imagine He would care either.

The reason why I'm telling you this is that some people back then did make it, and they did even more drugs than we did. It was the early nineties, and singers whipped their cocks around microphones; they drank and threw up in cabs. The girls from the Art Institute stripped and never wore underwear, even after work. They lived in a perpetual state of early childhood—skipping that preadolescent angst that I had gone through, where I was stuck: feeling responsible for my mom and dad, but not taken seriously by anyone.

Around the time I bought the rhinestone pants, Ebin and I were fighting more than usual. He wanted to make the bus a commercial enterprise and compete with the mariachi buses that took late night parties around the Marina and the Mission. Theirs had painted sides and velvet paintings on the inside, and the mariachi bands were authentic, or sounded good enough for the drunks. But Ebin could never figure out what we would do with our stuff while we ferried people around. We collected books and flotsam and had nets and milk crates to try to hold all of it.

He drew all day, and I had to get the right permits from the city. He felt he could offer a new experience: a Ganesh statuary, marigold garlands, and Bollywood hits blaring from the speakers. But he was ahead of his time, as usual. We didn't even have a toilet. We had to put our crap in pockets of tinfoil at night and leave it by the docks at dawn.

I yelled at him that he was ruining my life. "I'll leave so you can ruin it yourself," he said.

When you live in a bus, you lose that urban propriety—if it ever existed. I walked around the city and couldn't hear much from the windows, but I'm sure people screamed at each other and broke things. I yelled on the bus and I yelled as he walked away, with a paper bag full of drawings. I ran down the street after him. The white sky glowed above telephone wires looped between concrete buildings. A parked car had its headlights on, shining on me, though it was still light outside.

Ebin didn't come back for several days. I tried to make the bus nice with handsewn curtains and succulents. I wrote poetry, filled out job applications. When he stayed away for a few weeks, I took a vacation from the bus, staying in the East Bay with friends relocated from Portland.

I got a job as a secretary for an alternative school in Emeryville, an industrial city between Oakland and Berkeley. One day at lunch, I found a metal shrine next to the railroad tracks. It was in shape of a human, with a feather-like headdress. The stomach was made of a metal camping plate, and it had a candy gummy fish as the belly button. I walked there with a friend from work. I didn't feel like I was cheating; we were just idling by the tracks headed north to Portland. He used to jump trains when he was young, and I suspected he put the shrine there to woo me. We picked a way around the broken glass to have our picnic. He said he'd help me with my high school GED.

I heard Ebin got a show at a Mission bookstore and all his pieces sold. I couldn't believe it when I stopped by to sell used comics. The owner showed me the receipts and the reviews in the free weekly. Supposedly a collector came by, too—one of those yuppies who liked to eat at the sushi places taking over the Mission, not caring about the parking tickets or the junkies begging for change.

But what really struck me was the piece that got the most attention. Ebin had taken my rhinestone pants, the white ones, and had handstitched a sinuous piece of red velvet down the side of one leg, like a lava flow. And he covered the pants with my stories, poems, and secrets. He wrote it in block print, like he was a crazy person at one of those art studios for autistic people. And through the words and the velvet were marching soldiers, unicorns, elaborate forts and weaponry, even a silhouette of the crazy Red Man. He didn't do it for me, or for our dead love. He did it for himself, for some strange vision. I thought it was hideous, but it sold.

WET

My husband breaks a slat of the bed I grew up in. It's a mahogany sleigh bed from the 1800s. The headboard is stained with handprint ghosts from our son's dreams.

My husband sets up our son's new bed and mattress. He let our son use a box cutter to slice through the shipping cardboard, and it slips into the fake black leather. A small gouge.

Say nothing.

I say something to the boy, the almost-teen, couched as an insult to the husband. He glares at me.

This is uncomfortable.

I go to my office, the third bedroom of the sad house. I have books and fabric scraps. I have dead friendships and active stomach bacteria. Famous people never email back anymore. Was I boring? Don't answer. Don't answer.

Yes.

I have stained teeth and an undeniable love of cheese.

If everything is out in the open I can see it, until there is nothing to see after all. Rectangular shapes and colors. Is it moldy? A closet full of secrets—but why?

I have a bad gin headache and many unfinished projects. I can't find Advil. Four coffee mugs and one espresso cup in bedroom. Fifty books I will never read. I have lost the sweetness, affection, lust, and pride in the other. I forget the pet names (but I remember). I give up the teasing (I transfer it to the cat).

I live with a polite stranger, a slob. I am a slob.

"Mealworms can be ground into butter. They taste like cow milk!" The top of my brain is pressing upward into my skull. It's my fault.

This Big D. Not the dick. The divorce.

I cut off my left arm with nail clippers. It hangs on. I can't snip the final pieces of dried-out skin.

The initial hurt: I saw it on my arm, too. "I'm in love with—." A flap cut into the shoulder. The cuts extend on either side, forming a bloody jelly roll. Not till death. Till legal documents coming through the email.

At night, I tuck our son into his new bed. He tells me: "You and Dad are divorced on SimCity." I was a grandmother on it, rocking the baby. That gave our son points. Now my boyfriend is my husband's roommate, a black guy.

Soon our son never visits that game anymore. Digital limbo. Soon I will never be married to my husband except in nightmares.

Our son asks: "Is sperm white? Is it brown like poop? Or yellow like pee?"

I say: "Ask your dad."

I cry in therapy. Divorce is violent. My husband. A nice person. Except when he swears. Except when he looks at me sobbing on the chair, on the rug. Anywhere. Our house is welcome to all tears.

Moths eat the felt pads inside the piano. Fleas jump on our son's iPad. Maggots squirm inside the sesame seed jar. Their perverse dance. I destroy my liver. I grow a mustache.

Our adolescent son screams. Now he's a toddler. Now he's an infant. He is in the womb. He's the cells that formed him. Does the egg scream when it's pierced by the sperm?

The window doesn't fit right in the frame. It's an old house with a lot of potential. Where are those clouds I made of carbon dioxide words, my greenhouse gas of hate? Do they form steam in the bathroom? I am cold.

My husband drives to the dump with the futon stained with pee and tears. He tells me he wanted to drive off a bridge. Two days later he leaves the country for a year. My son and I spin in our rooms. Two months pass. Then: snow.

"Mom, come out." The son, twelve, shirtless, in shorts and sandals. He runs into the night, now white, like a healthy uterus, its tissue open to life. Flakes cover the harm: the cat's grave, the thorns. The suburban failure machine. I laugh at the son for his snow dance, his delicious chaos.

I make a snow angel. The metaphor fails. The son stomps it out. No angels here, so we raise our tongues to the stars: we taste what melts.

THE COURTSHIP OF EDDIE'S FATHER

I get a ride with Ann-Marie, the mother-in-law, to the family picnic. She turns left from the road into Golden Gate Park, bullying the Honda over the curb, onto the bike trail, and toward the picnic area.

"Cool it," Ann-Marie says. She waves at me while she speaks, and her thin, gold bracelet nearly hits my fucking face. "If we get stopped, point out the cooler in the back. People drive to these picnic spots all the time. That's what the trails are for." She likes to be bad. She yanks on her skorts. Jenny, my wife, has a matching pair. She told me that a skort is shorts and a skirt put together. I am truly sorry to know.

I try not to look at Ann-Marie's tan, waxed calves, knees, and thighs, shiny with tennis buff. I slink down, shut my eyes, and stick my foot on the dash.

"Down, please," she says, nudging my thigh. I cringe. Mothers-in-law should not touch any of sons-in-law's body parts that attach to "privates." Especially when said son-in-law wears shorts and his mother-in-law touches skin with (I open my eyes) pale, silver nails.

A kid in a camouflage outfit stands by the trail, his feet outspread in the patchy grass. He shoots at our windshield with a high-powered water gun. Cherry liquid smashes against the glass.

I roll down the window and flash the peace sign, but the kid, no older than eight, raises the gun to shoot again. Ann-Marie agitates the windshield wiper. "Damn brat!" she says. I say nothing. I like his style. He could've been my kid, if I'd ended up with his mom, whoever she is, instead of Jen.

"So, we're here!" Ann-Marie says, once again thrusting me into family submission. "Do you see that woman? Crystal?" She slams the brakes on the grass.

I sit up and look for my wife and kid. I look for Crystal, our kid's birth mother. He has her smile.

Jenny walks up to get the stuff from the car. She looks pissed but maybe it's because she's not wearing her sunglasses. She has a natural squint. Her legs, though—just like her momma's. She's wearing skorts, too. Red ones. But her top is stretchy and tight.

The baby monitor had sputtered this morning with the animal whines of our child. Jenny straightened out so her butt no longer pressed against my stomach. I rose to fetch Eddie, feeling the ache in my lower back. The kid was crying, no doubt, because he wanted the soft plastic nipple of his bottle. I have Jenny's audacious breasts to myself—when I'm lucky. Eddie got to suck tit for only the first few days of his life, before we adopted him.

"Where's the baby?" I ask Jenny.

"At the children's playground—with Crystal."

"Did everything go OK?"

"Yeah. Her plane was on time," she says. I wait for more details, but she adds, "Why are you so late?"

"Oh, honey," Ann-Marie says, opening the back door of the car. "I was out of gas. Then we needed money."

"She forgot her card. We had to go to our bank," I say. I feel nervous, as if covering for something perverse and tawdry, but Jen can't read my mind.

"Jesus." Jenny turns to carry cups, napkins, and other crap to the picnic area.

"Is that a nice thing to say?" Ann-Marie calls after her. "This is our day, honey. Your first Mother's Day."

Gary, one of Jenny's brothers, steps out from the grill and throws a football at me. I duck, and the strings on the ball scrape my cheek. He's wearing a Cal sweatshirt with the sleeves torn out. He calls out, "Dude. Set an example! You don't want Eddie to grow up to be a wuss." I try to balance the football on my finger to impress him, but Gary walks back to the grill to man the tongs.

The chipped picnic table staggers with plastic bags and soda bottles. No one bothers to talk to me. Gary's new girlfriend looks good in her turquoise tank top and shorts, squirting suntan lotion on her arms. Gary and Mike—Jenny's other brother—fuck with the BBQ, and four of their kids use a jump rope to tie the fifth—the youngest one—to a eucalyptus tree. I feel bad for him. Those trees are sticky.

I sit at the picnic table, hoping no one asks me to do anything important, like find Crystal. I'm scared of her. I saw her intestines, after all. That's about as intimate as you can get with a virtual stranger. It was in the adoption plan that we could be at the birth, and she ended up having an emergency C-section. I almost passed out when they cut her open. Jenny, however, watched everything.

I take a fat Meyer lemon from a bag, slice it open, and squeeze it into a glass. Just one lemon produces about a quarter-cup of juice. I add bottled water, and the membranes float in the liquid. The seeds sink to the bottom. A genetic waste. We don't ingest and shit them onto the ground for procreation.

There's a shame in our marriage, and her whole family knows it. It sparked nice and bright at our first adoption meeting. Jenny and I sat with a group of strangers in a fluorescent-cursed room and chewed pepperoni sandwiches with extra mustard. Everyone grilled each other about who spent more on medical treatments, with the fat lady up front exhorting us on what fools we were to spend money on in vitro fertilization. "If I had a business where I'd take twelve thousand bucks from desperate couples with only a twenty-five percent guarantee they'd get what they want, why, sign me up!" And everyone talked about who did the pricking with the inch-long needles and who had the endometrioses and who had the chemical pregnancies and who had the mangled tubes and who produced eggs one by one, like a chicken. None of the guys with the folded arms copped to dead sperm, though.

We spurted out our tale: seven years of marriage and five miscarriages due to a pH imbalance. "They're all your children. You have to honor that," the lady said. We told them Jenny's body rejects my DNA. It rejects our fetuses. "But you're so young!" the counselor said. "You can adopt! We can help you," and she put a sticker with a baby's face on my shirt.

Jenny's body thinks those mini-fetuses are an infection, an invasion. She barely shows an interest in me anymore. The last time we told the family we were pregnant, one of Gary's kids, the delicate genius, leaned his head on Jenny's belly and said, "I don't hear babies crying inside you anymore." I didn't say that at the meeting. I can keep some secrets.

Jenny described how we went on as a happy couple, enjoying our annual trips to Carmel, and how I taught lessons at the back of a guitar store in Berkeley, but the lady interrupted her and said, "Then you felt something's missing, didn't you? You realized God has another plan for you." Jenny looked stricken. A true atheist. I got her a Coke. She swallowed her tears and turned pink.

After lunch, a couple came in with their baby, a crawling, squirming girl. The guy told us how he had bought a twelve-pack and sat in a hot tub the first night they brought the baby home, too overwhelmed that a person, their birth mother, could give up her baby so they could be parents. Everyone stared at the little girl as if to eat her up. But I looked at the guy. Later, I guessed he was half in love with their birth mother.

That's because it's happened to me. Crystal. She burns me. Makes me lean and giddy. And what's she doing now? Who's she fucking these days?

I hadn't emailed Crystal or called or anything since Eddie was born almost a year ago. She needed to deal with her grief. That's what the social worker said. We couldn't help her beyond sending a few photos. Jen stayed in touch. She invited Crystal to the picnic, even though Ann-Marie was dubious. Crystal still lived with her mother, who encouraged her to see us. Strengthen the bond. Holy shit. Too many times recently, when Jenny was at work, I held Eddie up by the phone machine and played Crystal's tentative phone message with the flight info. Eddie must remember the voice, during those long, wet months inside her. It comforted him.

And now, Crystal in the flesh, on the park trail headed toward us. I stand too quickly and bang my knees on the edge of the picnic table. Eddie's snug in a striped onesie, stuck in a front-facing baby carrier, and all I can focus on are Crystal's cutoff jeans and black hair. "Hi, Mommy! Hi, Daddy!" she calls, as if speaking for Eddie—her son/our son. She's been trained well by the social workers. She puts the baby carrier on me, adjusting the straps. She's close. And I stiffen, awkward, almost rude. I do a hug that pushes her away. Eddie's between us. He mews—squished—and I picture kissing her and putting my hands down Crystal's pants, lying beside her on the grass and tracing my tongue on her C-section scar.

I take Eddie out of the baby carrier, and I lie with him on a plaid blanket. He crawls away—our old game—and I pull on his legs. We're a little rough. It's OK. Crystal sits by me, her plate smeared with macaroni and cheese. She lies down, oblivious (I hope) to anyone except Eddie and me. She's got purple nails, bitten to the quick.

I sit up, embarrassed, and tickle Eddie, who fusses at me, as if he can tell he's a pawn. I almost say to Crystal, "We want another Eddie. Will you donate eggs for us—and they can go inside Jenny? And it'll be my sperm. And I'll think of you when I jack off." No, I won't say "jack off." It'll make me seem like an ass. But I don't say anything special to Crystal. I think of walking with her, with Eddie, and showing her the dinosaur plants in the park and the tunnel where the bad saxophonist plays. I think of walking with her somewhere, so we can fuck.

I look up at Ann-Marie, videotaping the bowls of Jell-O and whipped cream, and I want to scream, "So what if I want to fuck Crystal. Your daughter rejects me!"

If I could only inject Ann-Marie's libertine charm into Jenny, I'd be OK. I know it.

We say, "Happy Mother's Day," and Ann-Marie gets choked up.

Jenny takes Eddie from me, and Crystal and I go for a walk, ostensibly to get Popsicles for the kids. We are not in step. Not like I am with Jenny. I try to look into Crystal's eyes to see what I see when I look into Eddie's. But she keeps her head down, averted. Disco roller-bladers, spandexed bikers, and families cheering their kids on trikes fill the section of road closed to cars. They pour out across the pavement as if from a faucet of good health. I feel optimistic. I lead her up the path to Stowe Lake, and we walk to the pier. I can't think of what to say. A turtle slips off a log into the green water. I wish I could submerge myself in it with Crystal—or without her—I'm losing my chance. I buy her popcorn.

"You know what my mom said when I told her I was pregnant?" Crystal asks, wiping her nose on her sleeve. "She was like, 'Every victim has a key to her own prison.'"

"Do you believe that?"

"I don't want to think about it. Can I tell you something?"

"Sure," I say. "You can tell me anything." I calculate the age difference—sixteen years. That won't make me look like too much of a shit, would it?

"I don't think Jenny likes me. She thinks I'm a slut or something." She takes a handful of popcorn and drops the kernels into the water. Ducks approach, bobbing their heads. I don't tell her the popcorn is bad for them.

"I don't think so. She's shy. She's grateful for what you've done."

"But that doesn't mean she likes me. I even brought

a picture of me as a kid, you know, for Eddie later. She barely looked at it."

"Give it time," I say. I count to five and kiss her. My tongue tastes buttery. I rub her back and draw her to me, hard, but she looks away. She steps back and wipes her hand over her mouth, smearing her lipstick.

I apologize, but she says, "I don't feel well. You're nice. Your family's great. Please let it alone."

She doesn't seem to notice anything I've said. She never did.

At the picnic area, I get another hot dog, cursing myself, erasing Crystal's taste with grilled onions. My wife and Crystal walk off to look at the rhododendrons. I try not to think about what they might say.

I change Eddie's diaper, wondering if he gave me extra shit on purpose. He gives me a kiss, too. Open-mouthed, and I die a little inside from love-sickness.

I wipe off the onions and feed a piece of hot dog to Eddie. "Here's a bit of chemical meat for you, buddy. We need to make you strong." He hands it back to me, half-chewed. I pop it in my mouth. I'm his example, after all, and I need to show him I'm game for anything.

TEENAGE RIOT

Anyone who reads this without my consent will have a very sad week. Anyone can read this when I'm dead. ☺ ☹ But while alive—BEWARE! I know that won't stop you!

At youth group, Mom made tacos, and the other lady made hot fudge sundaes. I heard a talk on homosexuality and my question was answered.

In health class we watched slides on drugs (which practically said drugs were good!) and prejudice.

Mary and I went through the graveyard and wrote down neat names. Two people in a car stopped and said, "Fuck you."

I don't understand why people would want to kill, torture, or kidnap people or why accidents happen. I don't know which I fear most. I've been thinking all day just why I was born and why I'm going to school only to die in the end and forget everything.

All of the girls except me ran around the room with their tops off. I didn't because I thought it was gross!

At home I listened to my stereo with headphones. So neat! I could even hear the singers spitting!

My deodorant doesn't hold so that wasn't good, but I joined Forensics. In Latin, Ms. T told us about her wedding. Her husband is Jewish so her family kicked her out. The only person at her wedding was her Mafia uncle.

I could've killed myself today except I'd be forgotten too soon and that's the reason it's not worth it. P.S. Art is hard. New teacher had us draw his dead pet stuffed owl.

Looked in mirror. Saw that I'm ugly. God just as easily could've made me comely.

Last night my boil burst. Blood and pus came out a little.

Met Yin and Angi at the community center. A guy by the pool tables said he was in college. He was a real jerk. He wanted to change the disco station Angi was listening to, which was fine with me, but he kept saying to me, "Stop swinging your butt," and he hit me with his pool cue.

Can you imagine President Carter nude? All flabby. Bet he can't last more than ten minutes. If I married someone who got fat, there goes our sex life. Shit. I'd be smothered.

When I saw Rick I was as nervous as a "cat on a hot tin roof." It was as hard as before talking to him, and he was a bit bored. He said he had sex with other girls because, he said, "I know what I'm missing."

Spent the night at Denise's. We stayed up till 1:30 and crimped each other's hair. We talked about her boyfriends and her first experience "Frenching." She thinks it's gross. So did I at first. Depends who with, I guess.

Pink Floyd's "Another Brick in the Wall" is so sad. Like the song "Dust in the Wind." That's all we are. Maybe we need to land somewhere, or will we just blow forever, occasionally brushing into reality? I love life. Why, I don't know. My sister's bothering the shit out of me.

I'm getting involved in mucho things. All I need is people to party with, a boyfriend, a new body, and a better personality.

I accepted, reformed, converted to the idea that I'm the one who has to change and so with that in mind I braved the cold winds and harsh breezes with the thought that the sun will shine again. High school's better because I'm not expecting anything from anybody and the people there are not important. People who don't like me can go fuck themselves.

Lisa and I talked in the dorm room about boyfriends. I felt sorry for Lisa because her boyfriend's like a lot of guys I know back home. He has his friends—sells his drugs—but doesn't want to leave. He loves sex. He's totally unreliable—says he'll pick her up at eleven for brunch. She'll go by his house: it'll be locked, and the phone'll be off the hook. He won't wake up till four in the afternoon because he went to bed at eight that morning. She had a miscarriage and he wouldn't talk to her for three days.

Marcus went to a bar and stabbed the bouncer. A guy recognized him from the high school football team and went to Stuart and Vera's house to ask Marcus why he tried to murder a guy. Marcus barely let him out of the back room alive. The police arrived with a warrant, but they knew about the dogs and wouldn't go inside. Marcus escaped out a window and met up with Arthur to take him to Dulles Airport. That night, Stuart and Vera packed a suitcase for him, making sure his name wasn't on it. Police cars watched the house, so Jimmy left for Willis's. The cops were surprised at all the registered guns in the house. It's funny that Stuart and Vera have so much money in guns yet hardly ever use them.

My parents were very impressed by Willis when he looked at my Dodge Dart. He told me a psychiatrist came on to him at the hotel he works at. The guy wanted Willis to piss in his mouth (that was too weird—even for Willis).

I want a dog. I'd name him Fish. I want something to love.

FAIRYLAND

Cookie's mom had a boarder named Theresa. She was skinny, and her long black hair was combed straight and shellacked with hairspray. She liked to think of herself as tough; after work, she wore a black leather vest with jeans worn thin at the ass and knees. She cracked her jaw when she was tired or irritable. These were Cookie's observations, since Theresa was her main habit—her roommate, her de facto older sister, or as much of a sister as she would ever have. Cookie was fourteen and Theresa was twenty, but seemed worlds older.

The front door slammed. Cookie took off her headphones in the bedroom and went to the kitchen. She shut the window and got out her algebra book. She wanted Theresa to herself, without the neighbors hearing her sing, yell or break shit.

Theresa opened the trashcan and picked out a paper towel wadded with blackened crumbs. "You burned the toast again," she said. "I have an excellent sense of smell." She had come home from her old-school hair salon.

"All that cut hair I breathe in will give me cancer. When I get it, remember why." Theresa made fun of her lady clients. "They wrap toilet paper around their hair and sleep on satin pillows to keep their sets. They look good all week, yet look terrible at night." She looked at Cookie to make sure she was listening. Cookie shut her algebra book.

Theresa said, "I'd rather look terrible in the day and look good at night, wouldn't you?" She turned the radio dial from the public radio station where Cookie's mom worked to one that played Top 40.

Cookie felt embarrassed when Theresa talked about sex, even obliquely. Cookie watered the spider plants and picked off the dead leaves. She had to get through her algebra homework and didn't want Theresa to pick a fight. She sat by the window, which overlooked the side yard. They had tried to grow tomatoes last summer. What the slugs didn't get the dogs did, searching for garbage knocked out of the cans. Anne, Cookie's mom, was perpetually hopeful, and had tomato plants growing in coffee cans on the windowsill.

Theresa pulled bags of vegetables out of the crisper. "Come help me chop," she said. She tossed a knife. It bounced and landed on the stained linoleum, its blade pointed toward Cookie. They looked at the knife on the floor and then at each other. Neither moved. Finally, Theresa picked it up, complaining and slamming the cutting board down on the counter. "Never mind.

I'll do the chopping. It's not like my hands don't ache from holding scissors all day, not to mention my back. It's not like I'm not fucking tired."

Cookie counted to herself and prayed the mood would improve. Theresa had to make dinner as part of her rental deal. Theresa defrosted burgers for herself and Cookie in the microwave and made vegetarian soup for Cookie's mom, hacking off the soft spots on the zucchinis and tossing in limp carrots. "Onions and dried ginger," Theresa said. "That's the trick." Cookie grimaced. It sounded revolting.

The phone rang, and Theresa pulled the cord into the other room for privacy. Cookie poured a glass of ice water and crunched the ice between her molars.

After the phone call, Theresa brushed Cookie's hair, perhaps to make up for her foul mood. Her hands smelled of bleach, shampoo, and meat. She plugged in a crimping iron and forced Cookie's hair into accordion waves. Cookie leaned against her chest, happy for the warmth.

Theresa held the crimping iron in one hand and a cigarette in the other. A song came on and she sang with the lyrics, mocking them. "I got it on with one of them," Theresa said, meaning the band. "But I'm not saying which one."

"Did it hurt?" Cookie asked. Theresa might as well be called Tiny, because her legs were so skinny, loose in blue jeans. The rest of her body looked lost, too, hidden under a Rolling Stones t-shirt.

She laughed. "A little," she said. "I didn't feel hurt

till later. He hurt my feelings, the bastard."

"Did it bend?"

Theresa laughed. "What?"

Cookie didn't repeat herself. It was called a boner, but she didn't know where the bone went after the guy came. She often felt confused, but she refused to admit it. Cookie guessed Theresa would be happy to provide answers to sex topics from *A* to *Z*, but Cookie didn't want to know. She didn't want to picture it, especially with Theresa's hands in her hair.

Several years ago, Cookie's mom, Anne, had picked up Theresa, who was hitchhiking in Berkeley by the I-80 on-ramp. Theresa threw her pack in the back of the station wagon and sat next to Cookie. She smelled like lavender and cigarettes and some sort of wildness, like moss and ferns. Anne believed in the goodness of people, barring Republicans, and said Theresa's aura was golden, a positive sign. Anne's entire family, the Staffords, picked up hitchhikers, gave money to bums, or brought in strays, their version of American pride.

Anne had gone too far, in Cookie's current view, letting Theresa move into Cookie's room. They shared a futon on the floor. The stuffed animals were stored in the closet because they gave Theresa the creeps. When she babysat Cookie, she told her about her drug trips, sitting in her bed—their bed—with her legs tight against her chest. She liked to keep the light dim, with a scarf over the lampshade. Cookie tried to imagine Theresa's LSD trips by shutting her eyes so hard she saw white flashes, but nothing made her feel as Theresa described it, translucent caterpillars coming up on the bed and wanting to infest her.

In the beginning, Theresa had asked Cookie questions as if she cared about the answers: *Where is Atlantis?* "In the middle of the Atlantic Ocean. It's a circle, a giant city with a dome over it. Every single magical creature lives there." *Even vampires?* "No. Oh, yes. They live in the jail." *Are you going to look for it?* "Definitely. No way anyone can stop me." But lately, Theresa could be so unpleasant that Cookie slept on the couch most nights, or in her mom's room, when her mom was at the radio station.

Cookie ate her burger slowly, waiting for Theresa to come back from the garage. She didn't let Cookie or Anne in there without her permission. She got her way through sweet-talking or through long periods of silence. She brought in an armful of clothes and dumped them on the kitchen table. The wrinkled tops and shorts smelled like stale air and plastic bags. Cookie held up a shirt with ruffles down the center.

"Who would wear this crap?" Cookie asked.

"This shit will sell," Theresa said. "Help flatten it out and I'll give you a cut."

After dinner, they put the clothes on the back seat of Theresa's car, borrowed from someone—Cookie wasn't sure. Theresa wanted to sell the clothes at used places on Telegraph Avenue, but she took a turn and headed the opposite direction. She didn't give a reason. They drove to an apartment in North Oakland. Cookie rolled down the window to look at her crimped hair blowing in the side view mirror, pretending she could read Theresa's mind, that there was logic in these days.

Theresa's friend lived in an apartment with a laminated Santa on the door. No one had changed it—not in January. Not even now, in May.

In the living room, Cookie ran a finger along a Venetian blind, daring to see if it would cut her. "Leave it down," a guy said.

"Don't be mean, Marcus," Theresa said.

Marcus had long sideburns and a skinny face crossed with acne scars. He sat on a plaid couch folded out to a bed, the cushions placed vertically against the back of it. On the mattress in front of him were piles of latex balloons, filled with brown liquid, like chocolate treats.

A game show played on TV, the sound on low. Cookie wandered around the apartment, avoiding the man on the couch. Theresa disappeared into the bedroom. Cookie could hear voices from the room—and laughter—not the good kind. She found things in strange places: a child's ABC block on top of the fridge, a plastic troll in the sink drain. She wondered if a kid lived here and was leaving her clues.

In the bathroom, she pulled the shower curtain back. A duckling sat in the bathtub, not yellow and fluffy but an adolescent, with gray feathers. It moved its head rapidly. It stank and its water bowl was dirty. Cookie filled the bowl and set it down in the tub, wiping off her arms when the duckling flapped at her.

Marcus stood outside the bathroom door. "You like ducks?" he asked. "I don't think we've had a proper greeting."

Cookie's hands were wet. She wiped them on her pants. His dry hand touched the scar on hers.

"Oven burn?" he asked.

Cookie pulled her hand away. The door Theresa had gone into was still shut, and Cookie could hear her laughing.

"I'll wait outside," she said.

"You can stay. Have a soda. He coughed and patted her on the head. "Nice hair. Theresa's work?" He held out some grapes. Some were brown, but most looked edible.

"No thanks," Cookie said.

"Really? I'm harmless," he said.

Cookie blushed and took the grapes. "Tell Theresa I'm outside."

"Come back soon," Marcus said.

She shivered. She would never go back there. She left the apartment, wishing she knew the way home. On the stoop, she watched a couple of kids walk by eating folded pizza slices. It was one of her self-improvement goals: to meet a best friend. So far, she was unsuccessful.

She wandered out to a playground, eating grapes. She peeled off the skin with her teeth so the grapes resembled slippery eyeballs. The metal equipment was flaked with red and yellow paint. She climbed up on the monkey bars and hung upside-down, her arms dangling. She liked the world better this way. Her hair touched the dirt. But the blood rushed to her head, and she saw Theresa's legs with her arms on her hips.

"Come on," Theresa said. "I've been looking for you."

Cookie pulled herself up and dropped down, tossing the grape stems into a bush. She wanted to ask Theresa why she left her with that man, Marcus, and why she wasn't protecting her. Theresa was supposed to be her sister, but she couldn't articulate a way to say it without seeming meek.

"So you won't believe this," Theresa said, "It's so funny." She held Cookie's hand and pressed it close to their side. She leaned her head on Cookie's shoulder. The moon appeared in the blue like a hologram. "Look up," Theresa said, as if anything beautiful had to be claimed by her first.

"Tell me. What were you going to say?"

Theresa skipped over the sidewalk squares. "So I got us some money," she said. "Let's get ice cream. We can sell the clothes later. Don't tell Anne about our little errand, though." She frowned at Cookie. "You'll regret it."

In the car, Theresa told Cookie she had held a guy's limp cock in the bedroom. "'Wow!' I said to him. 'Wow! Wow!' Until he got hard and laughed, too. It was just a hand job. So easy. You could do it. It's as easy as milking a cow." She stroked Cookie's cheek. Cookie felt diseased, with some man's cooties on her. She flicked the door lock open and shut.

Theresa held a hand behind her back with the

other holding the steering wheel. She looked at Cookie while talking. She wouldn't tell Cookie what she had in her hand until Cookie guessed. The sky darkened, and they drove around Lake Merritt, its necklace of lights shimmering on acres of trapped tidal water.

Cookie loathed that game. She knew Theresa liked to steal from people's houses, things people wouldn't notice until much later, like a doll's brush or beaded earrings. It didn't matter what price it could fetch. It was like a variation on the game of Clue.

This time Theresa held out her hand at a light and showed Cookie: it was one of those rubber balls from the couch, filled with brown liquid. "It's liquid hash," she said. "The best use for a condom I've ever seen."

Before dawn, the doorbell rang. Cookie, like a ghost, wandered down the hall, believing it was her mother, who sometimes forgot her key. She walked by feel, her arms out to her sides, bouncing from one wall to the other, banging into framed pictures of sunflowers, one falling then another.

The porch light was on, but she couldn't see anyone outside the window screen. She felt blood dripping down her leg; earlier, she had been too ashamed to ask Theresa for money to buy pads. She had wadded toilet paper in her underwear, but was sure it soaked through. She felt like a gutted fish.

Someone banged against the door. She opened it and Marcus, the guy with the grapes, fell into the hallway. Under his coat something squirmed. Its webbed legs kicked.

Theresa appeared behind them. She took the duck into her arms and stuck its head under her bathrobe. "Ducks are gullible," she said. "Here, take it." She handed it to Cookie.

Cookie looked at the dried blood around Marcus's nostrils. She stepped on blood she had dripped on the floor. Like a girl in a fairy tale, every word out of her mouth seemed like toad's words. She stammered. "Should we-we get him help?"

Theresa led him into the kitchen and Cookie put the duck in the sink. She got out the first aid kit. Theresa hummed and opened a couple of beers, as if this were normal, this man, this duck.

Cookie went to the bathroom to clean herself. When she got back, Marcus seemed cheerful. "I stabbed a bouncer," he said. "I'm not sure how bad." He said he had a bad count on the drugs or something, but that wasn't the problem. The problem, he muttered, was this duck. He couldn't take it into the bar. People were laughing at him. Theresa shined a light into his eyes. His pupils were huge.

"Alcoholics like to keep their bottles close," Theresa said to Cookie. "Remember that. This guy, for instance." She reached into his coat and took out a flask.

They went into the bathroom and Theresa ran water in the tub. Cookie stared at Marcus, naked, with bruises on his ribs. Hair formed a *V* across his chest, and a scar ran above his navel. He had another scar down his forearm. He spat into the sink and got into the bath, leaning against the rim.

Cookie went to her mom's bedroom, shut the door, and wrapped her arms around her chest. She watched the seconds on the digital clock whir past, and each minute snap down and click into place. Marcus must have guessed who had taken the condom bag of liquid hash.

After sleeping a few hours, Cookie heard the front door shut. She looked out her door, clutching a stuffed bear. The kitchen light was on.

In the kitchen, Cookie's mom, Anne, poured herself a cup of tea. Cookie rubbed her eyes and sat at the table. "Is Theresa gone?" she asked. "And that man?"

"What man, honey? And why are feathers in the sink?"

Cookie wiped out the sink, as she had wiped out burnt toast crumbs earlier, always covering up for mistakes.

"I don't want Theresa here anymore."

Anne hugged Cookie, and said, "Soon. I promise." Anne squeezed lemon into her tea. Her brown hair, streaked with gray, was pulled back. She lit a joint. "Rub my shoulders, honey?"

"Mom," she said. "Just stop."

Anne had taken Cookie to meetings in church basements, with ministers in sneakers talking about liberal theology. She wanted to sponsor Salvadoran families, yet she didn't know the only so-called refugee they actually harbored had gotten violent over a duck.

"Get me a washcloth, honey," Anne said. She put

her feet up on the other kitchen chair and leaned back. Cookie laid the cloth on Anne's forehead, cool like she liked it.

Later that morning, Cookie went out to the garage and saw the duck under a laundry hamper. Its water bowl had spilled. "God-fucking-shit," Cookie said. She put the duck in a milk crate bungee-corded to her bike and made a makeshift trap with a sweatshirt over the duck's head and a rope around its body. The duck hissed at her, so she fed it corn puffs.

She rode past driveways where men in shirtsleeves set out dominoes on card tables and shouted out to her. She hated Berkeley. She hated the tube socks and incense sticks for sale at the flea market; she hated roaming the aisles with Theresa, looking for her drug connection in the food stall lines or by the reggae drummers. She hated the men who whistled at her and told her to smile.

She pedaled toward Lake Merritt, with its turtles, ducks, and grebes. Marcus's duck was part of her outlaw adventure. That would shock Theresa. On the north side of Lake Merritt, Cookie walked her bike up a slight hill to Fairyland's entrance. This park was Oakland's version of urban nature, evergreens growing by parking signs and bare spots on the grass. Cookie had outgrown Fairyland. The tiny amusement park was protected by barbed wire, as if it could keep out anyone with a good set of clippers. By the entrance, a concrete Old Woman peered out the window of her pink shoe, the color of Pepto-Bismol. She has too many children, Cookie thought, but she's smiling. My mom only has one but I'm not good enough. She had to get a fake one.

Cookie had outgrown the ice cream man, too. He had strung brass bells below the handle of the pushcart, and plastic bags hung from the corners for people's trash. Grime smeared across the white surface of his freezer. A boy wearing pajamas ate a chocolate Popsicle and stared at Cookie blankly. Chocolate dripped down his chin. Although she was by Fairyland, none of its magic helped her charm this boy.

By the shore, ducks and geese staked out their territory, crapping so much that no one put out a blanket to relax. She put her bike down and let the duck out of its makeshift trap. It flapped, trying to escape. Cradling it like a doll, she took it to the water's edge. She held its bill closed and stroked its feathers.

The duck hopped into the green lake, joining the other ducks. It shook its tail feathers and disappeared underwater, with air bubbles popping on the surface. Like bumper cars, the ducks moved smoothly, pedaling their feet through the water, yet never hitting each other. The patterns in their wake looked like the *V* shapes of migrating flocks, but these birds were too habituated to leave. Their greetings were guttural, perhaps territorial. Cookie wondered if she had brought this tame duck to its doom, or maybe its instincts would kick in. At least it would die with the sun and moon and tourniquet of Lake Merritt's lights surrounding it, and not under an electric bulb in someone's stained bathtub.

Cookie found an oak tree to rest against. She almost fell asleep, her legs crossed over her bike. She felt a ripple under her body, the slightest of earthquakes. It seemed to promise something bigger in life.

A Mexican—no, a "Latina," her mom would say—glanced at Cookie to see if she had felt the tremor. She nodded back. The woman was pushing a baby carriage, and she paused to tuck in the blanket, as if that would protect the baby from danger. Cookie dreamed of having a baby one day. Being a teenage girl was like being meat on a stick. Some girls she knew compensated by not eating. They grew so skinny that light-brown hair covered their arms and legs. Others ate too much as armor. Cookie wanted to get bigger through pregnancy, with the right man, a good man, creating someone who would love her purely and completely.

THE PASSENGER

A backtrack. A rewind. Not too far. Just a taste.

A moon curve lit my way. Punk kids were hanging outside an all-ages warehouse, and they held torn blankets as the newest fad. They sucked the edges, bleeding fireworks going through their spinal cords. Sparks shot out of their fingers and the soles of their feet. They knew more about their bodies now than they did sober, and what they learned scared them.

I used to be in a band with Royann. Before she knew I was back to town, I met with her in secret, in an aural land of phone calls late at night. She didn't know I was calling from across the river. The water lapped. It brushed against piers. It touched the fur of muskrats and fish died in it, suffocated by sewage, damaged by prescription drugs flushed down toilets. I couldn't hear the river, couldn't feel it, but I knew it gave me some protection. I didn't want to see her in person.

I called from a phone booth outside a Dollar Tree, its floor punctuated like a speech balloon of flattened cigarette butts. Its phone book was torn off the plastic holder, except for one page, on which I wrote fragments of our conversation with a pencil stolen from a bar. I put my finger in the metal slot, searching for extra coins.

"The electric guitar is not an instrument on its own," I said. "It's a relationship with the amp. If you plug it in straight, it's boring and flat. It has to be loud enough so the strings resonate, so there's a sympathetic vibration. You're never going to get anywhere with Connor if he has guitarists with a clean sound."

"No, he's moving away from that. He's got a new approach. He's a dick, but I think he's going somewhere. Danny quit."

"What's he going to do now? He has no life."

"He'll figure out something. They weren't talking toward the end. It was time."

"But you liked him," I said.

"We only slept together once," she said.

I didn't answer right away. I never knew if I talked too much, or maybe Royann's steady breathing and occasional grunts indicated a soulful understanding. Sometimes I didn't even know if she was listening. Maybe she put the phone down. Maybe she was watching the TV on mute. Sometimes I believed I could hear the bubbling of the aquarium, or was it the hiss and bubble of a bong?

"Are you still there?" she asked.

I was getting cold. I nodded, hoping she could feel that, but she said, "I have to go. Don't overthink music. Don't go on dead-end tangents."

I hung up, and picked it up again to hear the dial tone. It soothed me, as if it remembered the talk, her voice, her cadences, and could link me to her again.

Somewhere on this side of the river a band was playing. It didn't matter where. I found a show in a bar by a feminist bookstore, flashed my ID to the chick at the door, and waited in the back, so no one would talk to me. The room was long and narrow, with dark gray walls. Velvet paintings of women with blue-tipped nipples hung above the bar. The lamps on the walls were barely functioning and Christmas lights flickered. No heat. Everyone smoked, flicking ash on the floor or into pint glasses. Chicks in fake fur coats, guys with chain wallets and Carhartt jackets. A tribe of nihilism and overdrawn debit cards. Skullcaps, thermal shirts, and track marks. Like a downpour indoors: no one talked to each other. No one looked at each other. Everyone was pasty white. (No wonder Royann—whose mom was black—had contempt for us all: if she were here, she would spit as she sang.) No stage for the bands, though. The monitor speakers were like bulwarks, but not for long.

The singer was goose-stepping on the bar. He sang in bundled vocal complaints and yowls of off-key obscenities. He knocked over people's drinks, kicking them into people's laps. They lunged at him, but he'd shimmy out of their way.

I walked closer, passing the few people left. I wanted to be near the singer. I wanted to feel something. I could punch myself in the face and it would mean nothing. Would someone hit him? I wanted to see. It's not like I was a sadist or even a masochist, but the singer couldn't keep time, couldn't sing in tune, yet you couldn't not watch him. His skin was white and greasy, and his chest was covered with tiny cuts, like he slept in rose bushes.

The drummer pounded on the toms—his fills copped from AC/DC's greatest hits—and the bassist examined his fingers on the frets, or grinned at the audience, his teeth held together with meth glue. The guitarist created a screechy high end through distortion pedals lined up as in a bakery display case. He stared like the pain he was transmitting through our bones would make us all feel better in the morning, the ringing in our ears like the sting of a venereal disease.

You wanted to believe you'd lived through something. That the music wasn't empty. That the muscles and blood and skin were put together for some reason beyond a pissing match between a bartender and a singer with a chipped tooth, now breathing heavy, now punched in the stomach by a skinhead.

I didn't mean to sleep with her. I needed a place to stay. She looked like me. We had the same colored eyes, brown, and we each had a mole on the inside of our elbows. I licked her eyeball to see what she'd do. She didn't flinch.

But that didn't mean we needed to sleep together. I was lonely for Royann. And this chick, she said, "I'm high. Can you take me home?" And she said it in such a fragile voice. I didn't have to tell her anything about me. She seemed to trust me. She told me her name was Jolene. Who was I to question her fake name to my generic "Joe"?

She pointed out the sound guy. "Don't look at him at the same time I do." She leaned against me. He had a scarred face, from acne, and deep-set eyes, brown hair that loped over his face. I recognized him. He was good at his job. He put his hair in a ponytail to work, and didn't care how stupid he looked. He was supposed to mix the opening band lower, so the headliner would sound better, but he didn't follow that rule. He waited to see if the opening band had anything to offer. He knew them through drugs. If they could talk to his drugs, they would get good sound.

The sound guy stood behind the board, with wires linked to boxes linked to the direct boxes, to the mics and amps and monitor speakers on the stage.

"He gives me money sometimes," Jolene said, about the sound guy. "Sometimes I put it in here." She pulled out a purse she'd made from under her dress. Her skin smelled good, even dressed in smoke.

"I need you to walk me home," she said. "My bones are softening."

I got her out of there. She was wearing her Granny's party dress. It was black like her hair, and its neck was encrusted with fake jewels. Someone had tipped her over into a bad trip. She wouldn't say who. I guessed it was the singer. He had poked her chest and said something about death.

Jolene felt her Granny inside her, and she was pulling her down. The last time she'd seen her Granny she was listening to a Walkman, with the radio turned to a God station. Her Granny wrote many checks to that preacher. I shook my head in sympathy and put my arm around Jolene. We were the same height. We were the same weight.

I walked her home to an apartment one floor up from a dry cleaners, and she leaned against the kitchen table that held bags of chips, spilled salsa, and a deserted ant farm. I poured us water in coffee mugs.

We slept together, but I wasn't disloyal to Royann. I stayed clothed and stared at the votive candles lined against her windowsill until the flames died in limp wax. She didn't sleep either. She sat with her back against two black pillows and petted a kitten all night, still high on acid, still afraid to pee or undress or walk. Our feet touched each other but couldn't get warm. The orange kitten scratched her arms with its tiny razor claws and Jolene never noticed.

"I don't want to kill it," she said, over and over. I wanted to take the animal away from her, but was afraid she'd hold it tighter.

She knew her bones were dissolving in her body. I wanted to know that feeling, to put it into music.

THIS IS NOT A LOVE STORY

No eye contact. No eyes. Dragged across the floor. Dragged across the carpet. Kicking legs, trying to get free. To what end?

Nancy Sinatra on the stereo with her leather boots—until the record skips. No more walking.

Bubbling water from the aquarium.

Bent over the bathtub, greasy water. Scar across your stomach. Scar up your arms.

"You want coffee?"

She doesn't say she hates coffee.

Body parts disappearing into others. Blue walls.

Gloria thinks, Most problems you can solve with a cock in your mouth because guys are so stupid. Except that isn't her thought. She doesn't think in grammatical sentences. It's what she feels. She stands in the living room, by the deck overlooking the street. It's dark out. She pulls up her shirt and pulls off the electrical tape. She winces, turning toward the sliding door to make sure Ham isn't watching. The tip of the cigarette. Where is it pointing? He spies on the neighbors, he spies on her, and she spies on her ex.

Her ex: The obsession. She is trapped with him in a walk-in closet. He has nailed a fish to the wall. He is six feet tall. She is petite. She runs her fingers through his chest hair. She moves his arms out to be Jesus on the cross. He obliges her.

Now her ex has moved out, leaving her with Ham.

Ham works at an auto shop. They met because Gloria almost crashed on the Fremont Bridge. Her tube blew out and the inner workings of the tire ground together. She knows she looked wild when she got the car towed there. She had to give the driver a hand job because she didn't have money to pay. Her hand smelled like him. So did her jeans.

She is a right-handed hand jobber, with the left cupping the balls. Or she switches it up, looking out the window at faded ads for face cream or soda painted on brick buildings in Old Town, Portland.

It is her hands doing it. Hands that wash dishes. Hands that type. She can lose one and live. She can lose both and get metal pinchers attached. Who cares if she jerks off some guy in exchange for a free ride to the garage?

Ham doesn't see her. He sees her as an obsession. But her gaze is elsewhere: her ex has a roommate, who must want to fuck him. If she wants to fuck him, then the whole world must want to fuck him, especially the people she knows, the people in stores he frequents, and the people he meets when she's not around. She thinks, True. And this is the word in her mind.

"I love you," her ex says (in her mind, that's really what he said). "You're beautiful." Days later, he says, "You're glowing."

"I don't talk to strangers," she says, but he is no stranger.

She doesn't record what he says in writing and doesn't tell her friends, but lets the words drift over her body. Nail clippings spike across the dish on the side table. He gets a postcard from his mom. A pig on the front. He said right away that he used to go to nudist camps with his mom. He lived in a cult. There were movies made. Nothing she does ever really surprises him.

She wears a tiara. He likes it at first, then breaks it in half.

SOME WEIRD SIN

The first sin was assuming an intimacy with someone through a pager. Access to her fingers, pressing the buttons, watching the screen, choosing to be sitting in one place, close to a phone, until something happened. Waiting for the vibration, which immediately got him hot. It was a contagion. Joe had a pager. She had a pager. Therefore, they were connected. The pager was always listening to the radio frequency. Then that sin transferred through devices and decades to the cell phone Joe held now. Watching the spinning as he refreshed get mail get mail get mail get mail get mail get mail. He twisted a piece of his sideburn into a tight coil. The last ice cube melted in the scotch.

On the shelf was a glass stained red, ant bodies stuck in the crust. From his son's strawberry milkshake, which he'd made himself. As if cooking made him a better dad. His son had watched him scoop the vanilla into the blender. He said it looked like an iceberg floating in a bloody sea. His son usually ignored him.

His son with his spattering of freckles. The shadow of dark hairs above his lip. Not quite a teen.

As a kid, when Joe sat with grownups, they talked fast and white spittle formed at the edge of their lips like the crud of polluted streams. He walked to streams to feel inspired. Like nature would tell him something, but he found a condom wrapper. He found deer droppings and a pale salamander that didn't have the strength to pull itself out of the water. The water flowed over a sideways deer corpse, its eye brown and cloudy.

Then Joe changed, fell in love with a young drummer, and had a device that tied him to her. Not his wife. Even his wife couldn't say her name, because it would give her a magical presence. Joe wanted his wife to say her name. He prayed she would.

Deer die off of strange diseases now.

His fantasy involved playing guitar in a British band; the slur of a British accent was unpretty, hard on consonants, dragging vowels down, as if grit meant honesty. Seeing the outline of a cock in Robert Plant's pants: he could do that. Instead, he heard the rub of a cat paw on the sliding glass door, so innocent, as if the cat hadn't killed something outside. As if it could deny the bird feather in its whiskers. Musicians weren't unemployed. They were in-between shows or tours or recording or practicing. But he did spend a lot of time letting the cat in and out. His wife never thanked him for that.

Before he got kicked out of his band, he tried to get them on a tour with...he won't admit who the band was now. They're assholes, anyway. He reached out, clawing on the chick drummer, not peeing submissively, but emailing her links to small-town crime pages. The desire was one-way. He was like a concave-chested teen with samples on his iPhone that he recorded into a four-track, then played out into a basement tricked out with baffles made of old foam from under the futon. He forgave the drummer for liking Faith No More, Pearl Jam, and the Dandy Warhols.

He wanted to play her a perfect guitar line. He thought every nipple would taste the same. Not true.

A band's emergence into an entity happens through layers of wet strips drying, with B.O. replacing the odor of papier-mâché goo. All those hours in a van together. Stale fart air, potato chips, cigarettes, hair spray. The essence of a bar and a nursery school birthday party. Blood on the cymbals. He bragged to his band that they would go on a European tour through his connections with that drummer. They fired him through a text.

The walls of his home were sticky, coated with translucent patterns, from air freshener, suntan lotion, and his son's successful attempts to kill ants. There were remnants of hairspray and cooking oil. Trailings from silverfish and ants' microscopic licks.

Joe couldn't parent through benign neglect anymore. With divorce looming, he created the bad time. The hurt that was attached to his son's head. The ruined birthday. The inability to extricate child from house to hang with him. The back talk.

Joe heard his son talking to his wife. "Get me pizza. Pizza. Make it triangles. It's OK if they're not, but I want triangles."

"I'll try to get up but my butt's so heavy it might not make it through the door." She sang a song about her butt. He used to like her songs. Now they grated on him.

Moss crusted the roof and gutter. Another failed home improvement project.

The first breakup conversation with his wife needed subtitles. Everyone has had these conversations; even a monk might have one with another monk, scrubbing potatoes or polishing Jesus's wooden bones. The heat of the crotch against the mouth. Monks would know this.

There were gestures. There was snot and heaving. There was drawing squares and rectangles and triangles with crayons. And certain words. There were flashes of panic in the amygdala. Yes, memories would be made. Neural pockets died off, obliterated. The heat of someone on his shoulder. The arm. The hand. The averted face. The limbs were a substitute for that intimacy he'd found so quickly with his wife long ago. Then the limbs would be gone. He would see them only when his kid would be dropped off. A limb resting out the ledge of a car window.

Could I feel the loss of my inherent body, Joe wondered? His wife felt the loss of the body she knew well (before adolescence) by the addition (of fat), yet Joe had lost his inherent body (muscle). He had dropped fifteen pounds in the time he'd fallen in love. His loss was magnified by the body weight of the anorexic drummer he loved. Anorexics denied the desire to transform sugar and fat and protein into fat cells. Her desire: ultimately unknown. Perhaps not Joe. Perhaps never Joe. His desire: for her skinny ass.

Joe invited his son's best friend over when his wife was out of town. He set up the mini pool table from Fred Meyer's on the linoleum floor.

"All you're doing is winning."

"I'm playing the real rules. I know they're real."

"You can't make up fake rules."

"Yeah, whatever."

"Why do you even want an advantage? You always take advantage."

"You bad, son. You bad, son."

"The one thing that annoys me is that you always take advantage."

"Three stripes in the hole. You try to win. It ain't going to happen. LOL LOL LOL LOL LOL LOL."

The play date was a disaster. His son punched his friend in the gut. His friend hit him across the face with a Styrofoam sword.

Joe fought the urge to pick up his guitar and play, to ignore them, to pretend they didn't exist.

He didn't notice the plug came dislodged from the aquarium heater and oxygen bubbler when he finally extricated his son from the house.

When they got back, his son cried. The fish were belly up. Their energy dissipated into the water. The water forgot. It didn't have feelings. Even though his back hurt, Joe picked up the tank and emptied it. The water flooded the garden, and Joe assured his son that it would be good compost for the tomatoes they so loved to eat. He forgot he would not be there next year to eat the tomatoes.

"You asshole," his son said.

THE TENANT

"Your move-in date is in February," the landlady said. "Like whenever. But this is today." She pointed to a pink highlighted square on the calendar. She had white streaks in her hair, pulled back in a retro butterfly clip. She wore a fleece sweatshirt and an owl pendant and jeans tucked into her boots.

The tenant nodded, without committing. This woman's accent, the tenant decided, was Dutch, which probably meant habitual awkward cheek kissing, as when they first greeted. But it was desperate Craigslist times in Portland.

"I can have movers come into my house," the landlady said. "That's all that I'm asking. But I need to prepare—get you a key." She emphasized the last word as if doing the tenant a favor.

The tenant sucked the cola and put the end of her straw against a piece of ice. Not sure if she should drink alcohol. Thought about how wet her underwear was. How it was nasty, but human. All women get wet sometimes. She won't mention her girlfriend. She hadn't even mentioned her girlfriend to her ex-husband. What's the point?

"If you want my help let me know. I can't be available twenty-four hours a day. I will make sure there is space for you to move in."

Behind the landlord's head, a TV. The hockey player was talking, the stick in front of his face.

She watched a man coming out from the bathroom. There were certain things old men did that her ex hadn't adopted yet, like stick his forefinger in his ear to clear out wax or pick the front of his trousers, or walk with arms separated from the sides, not swinging, like he was holding up imaginary baguettes.

The landlady tapped on her plate to get her attention. "Do you feel pressure? I feel pressure. I want to confirm this. You've been distant on the phone. Can we use this dinner to pick a move-in date?"

Her ex thought he could control his life. He spent hours studying the postal exam book so he could deliver mail. He timed himself with a metronome to mark progress.

The landlady moved into focus. She had a hair on her chin. "If you were going to lock your door, I'd need a key."

The tenant nodded, wondering if she could go into the bathroom here to swab out her underwear. But she didn't want to seem like someone who peed a lot.

"You need to tell me weeks in advance when you're going to move out. I will never go into your room to borrow your shoes or borrow a pair of scissors. If I was stupid enough to go into your room to steal your shoes." The landlady was finished with her second Chardonnay. Hadn't touched her burger.

The tenant looked at the men in the bar. They put their hands in front pockets. They kept their hats on, even indoors. They licked their lips. And now she was trying out this other thing. Women. Why not? Her parents were dead.

Men let dates dip their fries into BBQ sauce. Men brought their laptops to bars.

She'd met the girl, the girlfriend, the night her favorite band came to town from Chicago. She'd leaned against the stage, her head back, slapping the tape-covered wood with her bare hands, giving it the best hand job she could, the vicious kind. And the band members looked down at her: the guitarist stepping on his foot pedals, the singer spraying spit from the microphone, changing rhythms and singing in a half-spoken, half-melodic yelp to get his political messages out, never mind they couldn't hear a thing onstage, all deaf from blown-out cilia.

Some kids from college waved hi, and she slowly took off her clothes in the club, copying the action of this older chick, who by the end of the set was kissing her. Her name was Margo. Her tongue easing around her mouth like a happy clown setting up a joke. They made out everywhere and the tenant rarely ever had to use her hands, since the girl preferred to hold them behind her back. Or twist her nipples. Somehow she got her clothes back on. Or someone's. Most of her own.

Margo hooked her arm through the tenant's and spun her around, slammed her into the punk boys kicking up their legs like a herky-jerky roulette wheel. They were pretty boys, especially the black and Asian punks with bandannas tied around their legs, flannel shirts around their waists, one dude with a lightning bolt shaved into his scalp.

The tenant went into the bathroom with Margo. It seeped water in the corners and dripped water from the pipes. Wads of toilet paper stuck to the ceiling as if the tenant were back in middle school, hankering for a place to smoke.

They spent the night together. Margo seemed bipolar or a little crazy or a little out there. She was the purple to the tenant's pink. She was dark purple like a Siouxsie Sioux album, eyebrows drawn in black and angular and purple eyeliner mixed with yellow, like a perpetual bruise. She had a slash of red over her thin lips and wore tank tops loose on her, the armholes too big, showing her stash of armpit hair, her Chia pets. She had pierced nipples, but didn't brag about them.

The waitress asked, "Do you want another soda?"

The tenant looked up.

"No, she's had enough," the landlady said. "All that sugar." Shook her head. "You need to clean the backyard so it doesn't stink of dog poop. Then there's the kitchen, dining room, garbage, back yard, BBQ pit, and bathroom. Don't let the canister get too full. Don't leave the empty plastic bags full of cookie crumbs out with one cookie left. Don't leave the scrubbing sponges in the shower." One night had turned into five. The tenant couldn't wait to see Margo again. She loved the name. It tasted right. She had to get through this meal.

The landlady said, "About the kitchen: we each have one shelf. Do not add dishes. Clean the floor in front of fridge," she coughed, covering her mouth. "Oh, and cleaning the sink: if you make potatoes and bacon: I'm still going to clean it if it's my turn. I expect you to do the same."

The tenant's glasses were falling toward the end of her nose. She had stained teeth. Didn't care. But the damp underwear. Not good.

The tenant had spent days arranging plastic baggies of stamped crack bags into piles for a future art project. Then she found out someone else had done it first. So now what? She pointed to a date on the calendar, late in February, smiled and said, "See you then." She thought of the most banal actions of caged men. Yet how honorable they seemed compared to caged women.

OBSERVATIONS OF PUNK BEHAVIOR

I.

Dear Systematic Records: Please send me your catalog. Currently I'm here at a school to stop me from listening to Punk: But they won't stop me or break me!

II.

Rowan was one of the first punks with a mohawk in Austin. One guy worshipped him and fed him bong hits. At a party, he swung Rowan too hard on a hammock, and Rowan flew out and hurt his back. The guy rushed over and extinguished a cigarette on his own tongue.

III.

In San Diego, Marc had a friend who hung out by the railroad tracks with other hardcore guys. One day he said, "You want to see something really punk?" He ran out in front of the tracks and was instantly splattered. Later, his friends went back to his death site and found pieces of his flesh, which they kept in glass jars.

IV.

A punk chick yelled to her kid in the Haight: "Don't say 'peepee-head' or any of that other crappy kind of talk!

V.

My boss at *Mix* magazine said, "Punk is a bullshit attitude."

VI.

In L.A. I got a crush on Kurdt, the singer, because he spoke so passionately about this sleazebag named Courtney Love. He said, "I want to meet someone who's twice as jaded and intelligent as I am; that's why I want to have sex with her." But does anyone feel that abstractly about me?

THE GARDEN

At my co-worker's funeral, the minister invited people to share. No one did for several minutes, until one of the sisters stood up at the front. She announced to the mourners how her brother, whose real name was Charles, had gotten the nickname Spud. She was a short woman in her late fifties, with a blue dress and blazer. We had gathered in a Unitarian Church in Kensington, up I-80 from Berkeley and Oakland. Sunlight streamed through the skylight, lassoing my co-worker's photo, which was taken when he was much younger, perhaps happier. He had died of a heart attack.

The woman's hair curled at the nape, and when the woman turned to face us, I saw her braces, spackled over her teeth. She spoke quickly into the microphone set up by the photo and flowers, as if she couldn't wait to hide her dental work again. She said one night when they were kids, her brother had flicked mashed potatoes at her. The fork flew from his hand and pierced her cheek. I was sure she had spoken incorrectly, out of nervousness. She held her hand to her face, though, as if in pain. "That's how he got the name Spud," she said. "But we loved him."

I elbowed my husband, Phil, sitting next to me. The crowd tittered—perhaps to commiserate or perhaps in the hopes someone would come up with a more inspirational story. I couldn't wait to get to the food.

At the reception, I scooped up a bowl of Jell-O and made Phil get me a big slice of cheesecake, so no one would notice my greed. I sweated in my funeral dress, the one with the white pearl buttons. The church piped in show tunes from the 1940s—*Oklahoma!*, *South Pacific*. I wanted to plug my ears. Instead, I waved a plastic fork at Phil. It became one of our jokes—watch out for the fork.

I couldn't remember most funerals, but Spud's stuck with me. Since I was a nurse, I went to quite a few. The healing industry did that to you—wore you out emotionally and physically. I could be next. I was overweight. I also smoked from time to time.

A few months after Spud's funeral, Phil asked me to check on his mother. Apparently Adele had sounded confused on the phone, complaining that her neighbor was messing with her garden. On the Fourth of July, my day off, I drove east through the Caldecott Tunnel to Orinda. I took my stepdaughter, Margaret, with me. Adele cheered up around Margaret, forgetting that her granddaughter had ever been a drug addict.

Outside Adele's house, a low-slung condo, I found

the video camera. It was aimed toward the raised garden bed. The camera was Adele's idea. Phil had installed it the week before, drilling a hole through the wall and showing his mother how to retrieve and watch the surveillance tapes.

The sun bore down. I cinched the string of my sunhat and adjusted my pants. A few spindly sunflowers emerged from the soil; their seed casings clung to the leaves. The lettuce and carrots sprouted in haphazard lines. The carrots bunched together, with no room to grow. I pulled out white carrot tendrils and placed them on the frame. I felt sad for the ones I killed prematurely, like tiny carrot abortions. Phil and I were too old to have kids of our own. Margaret didn't count. I was fond of her, but no real daughter of mine would've become a drug fiend, even a temporary one.

Margaret sat on the stoop, examining her face in a compact mirror. She was twenty-four, but looked much younger. She had wispy hair, puffy lips, and blue eyes. Adele rapped on the window, so I tugged Margaret's arm. "Come inside and I'll owe you," I said.

"Nora, I don't like the old-lady smell," Margaret said. She picked at her black tights. One had a run down the leg and into a white go-go boot.

Adele finally came outside. "Couldn't you hear me?" she asked. Margaret smiled at her. She had kept all her teeth, even on her former amphetamine diet of Jujubes and Circus Peanuts. She had big teeth like her dad.

Adele wore an aqua sweatshirt and matching sweats, and her gray hair coiled closely to her skull. When I hugged her, it felt as if I were caressing a birdcage. She rolled her walker over the paving stones to the corner of the duplex and showed me the camera, as if I would be delighted and surprised.

"I don't trust him," she said. She pointed to the house opposite hers.

Mr. Martinez, a short man in his late forties, sat on a foldout chair in front of his garage. He limped across the street. He stuck a red-white-and-blue pinwheel in each mowed yard down the block, but skipped Adele's.

"That smarts," Adele said. "He wants everyone to think I'm not patriotic." She called out to him, "I'm American, too!"

He stiffened his shoulders, as if he couldn't hear. She pointed to the vegetables I had placed on the garden frame. "Look what that man has done," she said. "He's pulling out my garden. He's even bringing snails over to eat what's left. I have proof." Her German accent became more pronounced.

I fell back to my nursing persona: the detached voice and the soothing gestures. It made me lonely, but what could I do? Adele, a war refugee back in 1942, had come to California by way of Berlin and Amsterdam. That was not to excuse her paranoia, but it gave her depth. All of her high school friends had died in the camps.

We went inside, and Margaret got a cigarette from Adele's carton of Larks. She lit one for her grandmother, then one for herself. I felt a headache coming on. I brought a tray of Pepperidge Farm cookies from the kitchen into the living room. It was dim and chilly, with shellacked ducks on the side tables. Adele was losing her taste for food, or maybe she was going blind. In any case, she craved sweets, but her clothes hung on her body. She sat in a chair with high, thin arms. The fabric shone from the oils of her hand. She told me to bring her a plastic cup from the bookcase. A black snail lay at the bottom.

"Snails don't cross streets," Adele said. She pushed up her bifocals. "See that white spot? That's paint on the snail. Did you notice the fresh paint across the street? When I sleep, Mr. Martinez carries snails over in a pail. They'll eat my lettuce."

Margaret looked at the snail. "That does look like paint. Or nail polish."

"You're not helping," I said. "Can't we talk about something pleasant?"

The ceiling fan collected cigarette smoke and spread it across the room. Adele buried her cigarette butt in a portable ashtray and snapped the metal top. After biting a ginger cookie, she sipped her water so carefully her red lipstick never darkened her teeth.

"Take a look," Margaret said. She picked up the remote and rewound the videotape. I expected something shocking, a clue, perhaps. Instead, we watched a squirrel running past Adele's garden, in black and white. I asked her to replay it, as if watching a nature documentary.

I wanted to do right by Phil's family now—his mother and daughter. In the courting days with Phil, I believed I had found someone to trust. He held my hand tightly and listened to my complaints about unfair hospital regs and endless nursing shifts in the ER where I drew labs and started IVs. We went to Giants games, with me huddling under his coat—I never brought enough warm sweaters—maybe on purpose. I liked the way his coat smelled.

His daughter's addiction, however, nearly broke us. A lot of my fellow nurses did speed or whatever else they could gobble, so nothing shocked me. Nevertheless, we had to kick Margaret out of the house. For months, Phil drove by the West Oakland BART station, banging on the doors of two-story tenement apartments, the ones boarded up and patrolled by stray dogs and winos. Margaret couldn't come back to our house. I made sure of that. When she went on a meth binge, she covered her closet door with pencil dots. She stank like cat piss, and I could see through her lies. Her boyfriends were even worse. Thieves, all of them. I forgave her, but she carved a black space in our marriage.

Eventually Adele yawned, needing her afternoon nap. Her cigarette drooped between her fingers. I turned the VCR off and tucked an afghan around her.

I drove Margaret home. We closed in on the dark Caldecott Tunnel, due west, and I waited for her complaints.

"I can't do it. Don't go this way," Margaret said. "I hate tunnels." She pressed her knuckles to her forehead and rocked against the headrest. I turned on a Johnny Cash CD, thinking it might relax her.

"Turn it off," she said.

"Hold your breath," I said. "It'll go faster." Stained tiles and closed tunnel doors slipped by our windows.

I knew her fear. Nine years ago, in 1982, a truck had blown up in the tunnel. A fuel tanker created a firestorm when it smashed into a stalled car going westbound. We lived in the Bay Area, so it was our civic pride to note natural disasters. This one had primary elements: fire, rock, air, tears, and alcohol (a beer truck got destroyed, too).

When we reached the sunshine, Margaret exhaled. A red-tailed hawk soared above the rolling brush and canyons. "I saw Mr. Martinez in the window when we were leaving," Margaret said. "He gave me a nasty look. I think Adele's right."

"Nonsense," I said. "Next time we go there I want you to call her 'Grandma.' It's more polite."

Margaret fell asleep, needing naps like Adele. I glanced at her for signs she was using again—unusual rashes, muscle spasms—but her breath was even; she seemed peaceful. I turned on Johnny Cash again.

In October, after a night shift, I drove toward our home in the Oakland Hills. I saw flares of orange in the grass: small brush fires. Later that morning, Phil chain-sawed eucalyptus trees by our driveway. Their trunks bent down, splayed as if a giant had stepped on them. He sprayed the roof but I stayed in bed. I was too exhausted to evacuate. But when I pushed open the windowsill, the air reeked of eucalyptus sap and smoke. Behind our house, trees exploded. Like a perverse tennis game, they volleyed embers toward our wood-shingle roof. I pulled my shirt over my mouth and ran out to Phil. He told me to pack our cars, mine first.

I wanted to sleep. What would he think if I had told him I had stopped by Adele's house after work, sticking Safeway carrots in the ground to fool Adele? That someone was attacking the garden? That someone had cut the wire strung around it?

Phil used his thumb to create pressure on the hose. Around us, I was sure our neighbors were doing the same thing. It was hopeless. "Get the big ladder," he called. Blood thudded in my ears and my eyes watered. The wind tossed the Halloween scarecrow from our porch to the driveway. In the house, I picked up the laundry basket on the stairs. I threw in photo albums, granola bars, and a parakeet cage. Who knows why?

I ran outside and the hot wind blasted me. I heard bullhorns but I couldn't make out the words. "No, the ladder," Phil yelled. "Then the computer! What the fuck." I cursed him back, but followed his orders. In the basement, I unplugged the cords, hoisted the computer and monitor in my arms, and hit my shin on the basement stairs. The smoke alarms in the house pierced the air.

I wet a kitchen towel and put it around my mouth. Phil called my name again; his voice sounded hoarse.

I filled the cars with armfuls of crap. Why had we ever bought so much stuff?

"Drive out now," Phil said. "I'll catch up." His face was lined with grime. I held onto him because the smoke was so thick. I felt he could help me make sense of this terrible thing. We kissed and he curled my hair around his finger. "I'll see you soon," he said. I had been with him so long I rarely saw him clearly.

After the firestorm, I stayed with Adele. I had driven slowly down the switchback roads, offering rides to neighbors fleeing on foot—only one person joined me. It was faster to run. I tried to get to the Caldecott Tunnel, but the fires leapt across it.

Two thousand vehicles, most of them empty, had burned to their metal cores. Almost three thousand houses were destroyed. Emergency personnel found Phil's body in the rubble of our house. I didn't let Margaret or Adele come to the morgue. I wanted to protect them. And now I couldn't sleep—I didn't want to. I lost twenty pounds; they called it a widow's diet.

The insurance adjusters made me meet with them once at the property. I stared at the paper in their clipboards and crunched ash on the concrete foundation. Across the hills, chimneys stood by blackened trees. If they could be left alone, they would be happy, but the hills rumbled with bulldozers and earthmovers. I wanted quiet. I had Phil's name in my mind and it wouldn't shut up.

I remembered the orange and gray sky. Ash had drifted west across the bay to San Francisco. Ash made of people's bank accounts and bills and love letters and books they meant to read—in some places, it was almost an inch tall. The ash didn't need bridges or tunnels to get where it wanted to go.

In Adele's garden, the sunflowers were translucent against the blue sky. The center pockets held tightly packed seeds. The tomatoes overflowed and covered the pumpkin vines. One day, I picked all the lettuce, pulling up so much dirt that the salad tasted gritty. Adele stared at videotapes of her garden as if she could see Phil's hand in them. Dozens of tapes sat on her shelf, marked by date in red magic marker.

One morning in December, two months after the fire, Mr. Martinez greeted me. I wore a pair of Phil's sweats that I had saved from the fire and one of his baseball caps, the one that said, "Best Dad." He asked, "Are you going for a jog?" His English was halting, as if rocks filled his mouth. We sat on the curb and he handed me a can of beer. His hair had a purple tinge over the white. I let Mr. Martinez put his hand on my knee, because my grief didn't scare him. He had grown up in the Philippines. He told me of his war, Vietnam. His cousin got hit by mortar fire and lost half of his face. Most of his body was burned. In an intensive care unit in Saigon, Mr. Martinez smothered his cousin with a pillow. It was the softest way to go.

That night, while Adele and Margaret slept, I bleached the tub, the toilet and the sink until my fingers and hands puckered. The chemicals irritated my nose. I wanted the white shine and gleam.

Margaret slept on the couch, lost on Halcion. She had a Cal Berkeley football blanket on her, as if she were a sorority sister and not a former addict. Barrettes snarled her hair.

The TV was on mute but cast some light. I dropped the garden videos in a laundry basket.

Outside, I stepped over strands of wire fence around the garden, crushing cherry tomatoes and soggy pumpkins. I dug up tomato vines and sunflowers whose heads dipped with rot. The roots of the sunflowers bulged with dirt, all that effort for a brief gasp toward the sky.

Caking my hands in the soil, I buried the videos, ripping out the tape and draping it over the frame, as if I were dressing a mummy. Across the street, a light burned in Mr. Martinez's living room window, but I couldn't see a face.

WHAT DO I GET?

"Don't cheat."
"Don't squeal."
"Don't influence Gannon."
"Don't be a poor sport."

Meanwhile, you dampen your son's obvious glee in having a boy in the house who never criticizes him.

The arm is a lever. It is wearing out.

What do you want to know?

The open secret of who wrote Kim Gordon's bestselling memoir.
The open secret of rosacea.
The secret of a singer's dad throwing her across the room when she was a girl. She slammed her head into a bookcase.

The secret of money management, of a neighbor earning $85,000 a year in retirement.

The secret of postponed vacations.

of airplane books.

of stomach aches.

of being a man.

of stacked kung fu drums that will never be played.

of gay sex. The boy thinks the men do sword fights. "'Luke, I am your father.' They have sword fights and Darth Vader kills Luke with his light saber/penis."

of virginity (of not remembering being a girl).

of not moving muscles, of craving sugar, of wanting to know who the dead people are, the unclaimed.

of songs Amy Winehouse never sang, and bottles she never drank.

of waiting for emails that never arrive.

of lack of sex, the absence of knowledge of another person's body (was it the coughing, the snoring, the farting in bed? the softening, the hardening, the odors of decay? the musical entropy?)

of broken amps

of long-term unemployment.

of YouTube stars.

of the need to work and not being able to enjoy time with your son.

of moldy food.
of tulips.
of lies, the lying child. He lies to protect himself from judgment.

of a criminal sibling.
of dementia, of sitting in a chair all day (thousands of dollars of sitting, hundreds of thousands each year, a million or so).

and June asks, "Where is John?" She forgets her husband is dead, and her son has been on *America's Most Wanted.* She watches her friend's dog lick up fallen ice cream. The atrophied body after years on the tennis court. The missing teeth. Before she lost her mind she said to her friend, your mother, "You can get that shot that makes the ball drop cold."

the secret of beer.

of pubic hair behind the toilet, or to the side.

of staring at a pop star and imagining he can see you.

the faint bell of a cat.
the hum of a furnace.
forced air, uncleaned, filters, all your dead skin, pounds of it, circulating in your lungs.
the neighbors who heard the screaming and crying and tantrums (not so secret).
they don't talk to you.

you are an inner system of consume and produce, waste in and out.
dusty mugs at the back of the cabinet.
dark stain by the front door where the cat rubs himself.

how has the micromanaging served you, when you want to please others and you mistrust those who praise you?
you wear out your shoulder.
you have a large house.
you have a cat who peers outside.
people who take risks ignore your emails.

the body fights itself, or turns ninety-three and says, "I want a divorce."

A REASONABLE PERSON

Mary feels no relief in the courthouse bathroom. She should be used to this condition, three weeks into the trial—panic and a shy, clamped, out-of-order bladder. She has to go! She's hardly paid attention to anything the lawyers or witnesses have said all morning.

For days, she's tried not to pee here. She's waited until she and the other jury members were dismissed for the day. Today, like always, she wants her cushy toilet and her pale-blue bathroom, where Gladys, her guinea pig, watches her from her cage, and where the yellow-flowered hand towels are always clean.

She's trying to accept her reality, like her shrink advises. But these Hall of Justice toilets verge on ones from Mary's nightmare, because water from the plumbing seeps in the corners, predatory, wanting to despoil her overstuffed purse and knitting bag. Someone removed the coat hook from the back of the door, which makes the soggy tile more menacing. What—someone's going to steal from you here? It's a police department, too, for Christ's sake. But it's also a jail.

She clutches her long, puffy jacket in her lap. If the floors start to flood, she can pick up her feet quickly to avoid the water, but how can she wipe and pick up her bags without dripping pee down her leg or in her underwear? At least these stalls, unlike the ones in her dreams, aren't cut in half. The floors aren't black with greasy liquid. The toilet bowl she's forced to use isn't six inches tall and full of noxious fluids. And heavy metal singing sensation David Lee Roth isn't flinging his pom-pom of dirty-blond hair and dancing by the sinks.

Mary sniffs her armpits. Sad, too sad, but what can she do? She hears someone enter. She slowly unzips her purse and finds the smooth cylinder of her deodorant. She snaps off the cap. She puts the stick on her lap, on top of the coat. She can't reach under her turtleneck, which is tucked firmly into her jumper. She wipes it on the outside of her shirt. No one will notice; she'll put her jacket on.

"Hey, anyone have any extra TP?"

Mary recognizes the voice. It's chair number eight—Coral, the woman next to her. Mary sweats more. Should she admit she's in the stall? How would her voice sound? Pinched, confident, casual? Should she speak loudly, as if she's in another type of room, or in a normal tone? Could Coral sit next to Mary in the courtroom without thinking of her, hunched and debased?

"Hi, here you go!" she calls. She tosses the roll over the stall door, forgetting to tear off a supply for herself. Thank goodness she can use a Protecto toilet cover. She flushes, forces out a few drips, then flushes again and walks out. Coral hums in the next stall. Mary stays to be neighborly.

She checks her crepe-soled shoes. Dry. She looks at her face. Dry, too. She fishes moisturizer from her purse and rubs a white gob on the creases lining her mouth and forehead. No doubt her severe looks were a plus when she was chosen by the assistant D.A., a heavy-set, jowly woman—God bless her—in dark-pink tights and a dark-pink suit, who lobbed her easy questions. No doubt the defense attorney's desperation let her stay; the judge, D.A. and defense attorney went through about a hundred people to seat the jury.

Mary shouldn't have been selected because she knew someone who was murdered. The defense attorney sought her out based on one of her answers on the pretrial questionnaire. He called her by name, and she felt special. "Was the murder solved?" he'd asked.

"Excuse me?"

He repeated the question.

"No, it wasn't," she said. She laughed into her hand. "I said 'excuse me' because I thought you asked if the murder was 'soft.'" Then she sunk in embarrassment, leaning her head against the wall and looking up at the acoustical tile. Even now, she cringes. How callous. How disrespectful of the dead; poor Jerry, shot on the doorstep of his apartment after selling his uncle's stamp collection. He didn't need the money. He could've gone the next day. The guy beside her had groaned. He was shaped like a tent. He moved in his chair and tapped his foot. He sweated and coughed. He told the courtroom he'd seen his dad kick his mom while she was pregnant with his little sister. He was dismissed.

"Has anyone witnessed or experienced domestic violence?...Has anyone known anyone who was murdered?...Has anyone experienced or been affected by marital or sexual infidelity?" Mary had cringed at that last one, but she would betray nothing about her ex for her son's sake, even though he was selling Christ in Papua New Guinea.

"Can you scoot over, dear?" Coral asks. She looks at Mary in the mirror. They don't face each other. "Look at the bags under my eyes," says Coral. "This trial has made them bigger."

"I'll say," Mary says. She blushes. "I mean, I look tired, too. I mean, you don't look tired. I love your angel pin!"

Coral leaves quickly. Mary follows her, crossing the tiled hallway to the courtroom's leather door.

Mary likes to stare at the judge when she's not staring at her hands, her notes, the accused (so flat, like something to wipe away), the witnesses, the tile floor, the emaciated court reporter, the attorneys, the clerk (who plays computer solitaire for hours). The judge wears sweater vests but has the presence of Clint Eastwood. Mary wonders, on and off, if he's single.

This afternoon, Mary's a mute witness to bloody underwear. She can't touch it—not that she'd want to; she can only look. The blood is so familiar, from menstruation. Her mom used to cut out hearts from iron-on fabric to cover the brown stains on Mary's sheets.

In the crime scene photos, the blood is like a punch. The blood on the underwear, however, is muted. It needs an iron-on heart. But the heart would be too big. It'd be hard to buy an iron-on patch as big as the bloodstains, especially on the nightgown. Blood forced its way out of the woman's nose and mouth. It gushed through new holes. Death greeted her in a minute or so.

No one asks, "Who took the cat?" Mary saw the scratching posts in the photos and on the crime scene video. She saw the plants. Did they die, too? Who took her stuffed animals stacked on the TV set? Who took her Last Supper painting? Did the chrome mirror in the bedroom end up at Goodwill? And she tried not to cry when Rueben, the murdered woman's teenage son, spoke on that first day of the trial. But Mary cried anyway. They all did. He'd tried to prevent his dad from killing his mom. The accused stuck his foot in the door of Rueben's bedroom, where his mom had run for safety. She'd told her husband that day that she wanted to leave. He was too jealous, too crazy. That night he forced his way in. He grappled with his son. He switched the knife to his other hand so he could thrust the blade in his wife more easily. And the coroner, on the witness stand, confirmed the outcome, "Obviously, she had expired."

Mary pinches her hand to stay focused. She listens to a police officer with a broken nose. One time, her husband had lit his nose on fire. He was smoking a cigar and had stuck a toothpick in the stub. The flame caught on a tissue, which he'd stuck up his nostrils after he'd gotten a bloody nose. She stifles a laugh. The things she remembers in this courtroom! If only she could tell her son. He'd give her good advice on what's important, what will give her some leverage in the deliberation room. But she's not supposed to talk about the details of the trial until it's done. Until we reach a verdict. Until we nail the bastard.

We're supposed to look at the bloody underwear, the bloody bra, and the bloody nightgown without compassion or sympathy. We're supposed to view the video of the crime scene stoically. We're supposed to avoid eye contact with the attorneys outside the courtroom.

After the trial breaks for the day, she runs, breathless, down the three flights of marble stairs, skittering, sweating, her long, gray braid swinging against her sweater. She rushes by the security man, bulked up with a gun and walkie-talkie, and through the metal detector. Someone says, "Watch it, lady," and she pushes a bow-tied lawyer-type out of her way to hop into a taxi, where she urges the driver to turn up the all-news radio and hurry her home.

Mary overtips the cab driver and hustles up the

short path to her house. San Francisco's Sunset District is near enough to the ocean that she's surprised how often she forgets it's there. The fog edges over the roof and lingers by her potted ivy. Her house is small, but it suits her. In the hallway, she brushes lint from her quilted rainbow wall hanging. She made it while she was pregnant, thinking it would bring her luck.

She takes Gladys from her cage and breathes in her sawdust fur. She wishes Danny would come home. She's avoided his room since he went overseas half a year ago with his missionary group. His walls are still black—static black that hurts from the bad stucco job she did before her husband left. Well, she was mad at the time, understandably, and the stucco turned out a little sharp. The black is from her son's acting-out stage, before he became born-again. He insisted on the black rug, too.

Mary walks back to the living room and fluffs the pillows on her plush, white sofa. Gladys looks at Mary with brown dismay when she's returned to her cage. "Sorry, cutie, I'll bring you out later." Mary goes down the hall again, into her son's room. There's something she needs from it. Rueben lost his parents, too, and the jury, the sentient body, had to pretend it didn't care. She turns on the radio to a rock station that her son once liked. She reads the Christian books on his shelf, and they scare her. They're one reason she stays far from his room. *Occult Bondage and Deliverance. Demon Possession and the Christian. Angels: Elect and Evil. Victory over the Darkness.* He barely tolerated her the last few months he lived here. She pulls out a book, *Confronting the Cult*. Behind it is a squished plastic bag.

She pulls it out, holding only the outside corner. Inside lie a dozen or so condoms, unused. She drops the bag on the rug. So that's where they went. And she thought her husband had used them with someone else. She'd counted them regularly, always looking for proof. She sticks the bag back on the shelf, as if the condoms might burst out of their foil, inflate, and chase her out to the ocean.

She unfolds a pair of her son's brown dungarees and his blue- and white-striped workshirt and arranges them on the bedspread, as she used to do with his clothes when he was little. She gets out tube socks from his top bureau drawer and unrolls them, tucking each sock under a cuff. She starts to lay out a pair of boxers but decides against it. She knows her boundaries. She lies next to his clothes. She says, "Talk to me."

She lifts a sleeve and waves it at her face. She laughs. He thought she was silly, foolish, really. She jumps up and puts one of his baseball caps on the bed, too. She pats the knee of his pants and sits up.

"I found the condoms," she says to the pant leg. "Why didn't you tell us you wanted them? Or tell Dad at least? I thought he used them with someone else. You heard our fight. And it turns out there was someone else, eventually, as you know," she sighs, "but that's water under the bridge." After his dad left, Danny acted like he didn't care which parent he stayed with, until he was old enough to leave them both.

"You're bright. You're smarter than me. How should I vote when we deliberate tomorrow?" she asks his sock. "Maybe I can get sick. That's what the alternates are for. They're for people like me, who can't cope." She looks at the space where his face would be, but can't see him; she can't picture him. She gets up and takes his senior photo down from the hallway and puts it on the bed. She studies his wide forehead, his freckles, and his stern, thin lips. His eyes look kind, though. "Is your acne clearing up in the jungle? Have you met a nice girl?" she asks.

"You'd like the lingo at the trial. You were always a good one to pick up slang. The emergency people, when they look for injuries, they call it a 'strip and flip.'" Mary punches her palm. "I want to punish the guy. What would you do? He stabbed that lady, his wife, and his son saw. He tried to save her. She died in his room. Would you have stopped Dad if he really came after me—not yelled or sulked?

"Would you have run away? Ha. I guess I know. You ran pretty damn far from me!"

She stands and paces the room, acting like the teacher she used to be. "You'll like this—the science—or you used to like science, well, we learned how the lung functions and the consequences of his stab wounds. The pathways became open conduits for the blood. It came out the windpipe, out the nose, out the mouth. So much blood. The coroner even said, 'There were no other disease processes that could've contributed to her death.' Well, there you go. She looked so pretty in her driver's license. A sweet Filipina lady who had gotten up the courage to leave her abusive husband. Straight out of the headlines, right? And now what? What good will our verdict do? The son's life is ruined. He has no family except his paternal grandparents, and they didn't want him to testify. They didn't want him to bring shame to his family. They looked beaten, too."

Mary looks at the son she created on the bed. All she needs is straw or newspaper to stuff him with, then her neighbors would really think she was nuts. "I need to relax," she says. She draws a bath until the water storms the edges and the steam cradles the surface. She dumps her jumper and turtleneck on the floor, takes off her bra, and slips off her panties. She steps into the water, the heat searing her foot. She eases her body into the bath. Her breasts float and her knees stick up. Her toes pucker, but not unpleasantly. She folds her hands over her creased belly as if waiting for the judge's instructions: to be fair; to consider the evidence; to put personal feelings aside. The boy, the boy. She's sure the mother would never have wished that her death be witnessed by her fifteen-year-old son. Maybe he came into his life hearing her screams, too.

The prosecutor had asked him, "What's the last sound you remember your mom making," and he stood at the stand, his high school football jersey too big for him, and he said, "She was screaming." Mary rides her soapy finger down her stretch marks. She had screamed when her son was born. "No! I can't! I can't!"

The contractions had come too fast for her to get over the pain of the ones before. To her shame, her son's head made her rectum pop outward. She could feel it turn inside-out. She screamed because she thought she'd have to have a colostomy bag the rest of her life. She felt slit in two, ripped in half, and after her son was born her brown nipples cracked and bled at his hard sucking. But she forgave him.

Lust had made her son. She once owned that lust with her husband, who loomed over her and drove a cab and knew how to solder things. His low voice once led her beyond comfort and affection toward gnawing and lunging so quickly that she didn't recognize herself. She wouldn't want to. He woke her. She woke up so much that she couldn't look at their skin pressed together, but he found a way into her, cracking her skull against the headboard, so she lashed her mind into her body again. But he left because of her jealousy. She made a feast of it. She had more jealousy than the man accused in her trial, the one she could help send away for fifteen to twenty years.

After her husband left, she'd pull his stray hairs from a wool blanket they used on camping trips. And now she finds her son's stray hairs in odd places, like under the TV stand. She must be more vigilant with the vacuum.

Gladys is loose in the bathroom. She runs toward the sink, jumps straight up, lands, and runs toward the door. Popcorning. A happy beast. Prey. The phone is ringing. It goes to the answering machine. Then rings again. Mary dips her head so the tub's echoes comfort her. She'll consider the evidence at the trial. She'll put aside her personal feelings. Sure she will. It's what any reasonable person would do.

MY MARTIAN LAUNDERETTE

Troy paid attention, so things made sense. He stood on a metal stepstool, next to a rattling dryer. His back ached. He weighed 249 pounds (113 kg), which on Mars should have felt like 92 pounds (42 kg, a fucking nymph), but inside the inflatable space-colony dome, he was still huge, lumbering. Colonists were naturally nostalgic, and they had set up the space colony to replicate conditions on Earth, terraforming it with artificial greenhouse gases to make it habitable. No relief for a fat man. At the back of the Laundromat, Troy poked his hand through a hole in the wire mesh covering an air exhaust vent. Someone had inched down through to the other side and cut it out, hoping to steal from the coin-op machines. The space colony was crawling with drug-addicted thieves. All you needed was a clean brain scan to get here, and you could barter pharmas for a baby's scan from any orphanage on Earth. They always wanted meds.

On Earth's second day, God had separated the water in the air from the water on land. But on Mars, water was buried underground. The colony pumped and processed it, neutralizing the bad taste. And where water flowed, humans followed. The miners were drawn to the Laundromat not only for the promise of clean clothes but also for the steaming, sudsy water in the machines—it prompted saccharine visions of waterfalls and primal memories, when they were suspended in the saltwater curve of their mothers' wombs.

The Laundromat, painted Earth's sky-blue, had two aisles of washers separated by a long folding table. In the back were the dryers, stacked two high. About a dozen chromium miners, all men, were doing their laundry, standing over the machines with their eyes half-closed, humming to themselves. Their faces and hands bore the effects of heavy metal poisoning: mottled brown skin and dark pigmentation on the palms. Mars's thin atmosphere made the miners buoyant, and they gobbled serotonin re-uptake inhibitors to make them work happily. One sat quietly in a plastic chair. He must have wet his curls in a public bathroom and combed it down. It was greasy on top.

Troy stepped down from the stool, adding the air-vent repair to his mental list of chores, and swept up the ochre-colored dirt. The miners tracked it in, those nasty, poisoned folks with their constant vomiting and diarrhea, no wonder they needed the Laundromat so often.

Troy sipped a cola a customer had left behind. He frowned. He smelled rot around the can's sharp lip. Microbial rot. The supply ships didn't arrive from Earth too often. The colas went bad and no one fucking cared. He stuck his hand inside his pants pocket to feel his lucky pebble, his sacred pebble—the one he had found in the dust by a shredded bra.

He needed Bobbi's attention. She was slumped on a taped-up stool, her butt folded over the seat. She was eating her hamburger and French fries, as she did every day, as if her life as a Laundromat manager on Mars were one extended Happy Meal. She ignored his voice. But he needed her to unlock the office door.

Troy gripped his broom. He shouldn't touch her. He needed to. He shouldn't. It would be painful. The men needed taming on Mars, like anywhere, so to lure women to the planet, the colony leaders had installed electroshock machines. Men had to press red buttons if they couldn't control their base impulses. The leaders threatened uncontrollable men with expulsion to one of Mars's lumpish moons, like being sent to rot on a potato. Maybe a quick tap on Bobbi's shoulder? What was the harm? He did it, with the tip of a finger.

"Hit the red," she said. She opened the burger and licked a dab of ketchup off the bun.

"I need the tool kit."

"Hit the red."

"I did already. It's still working."

"You touched me. I can feel the imprint, the heat. Hit the red."

Troy reached above a dryer and punched a red button on the wall. It was about the size of his fist, like a miniature smoke alarm. The button beeped, loudly and steadily, as it adjusted its beam on Troy's balding head. He tensed his body, anticipating the currents penetrating his skull—300 electrical watts per pulse. Pain jacked his body, emptying his mind so he couldn't articulate the result: scattered neuron death. The watts penetrated the three layers of membrane protecting Troy's brain, all named after mothers, all vulnerable, whether hard (dura mater), spidery (arachnoid mater), or soft (pia mater). He fell, banging his knees and forehead on the chipped linoleum floor.

Mining was set up on Mars after it ruined Africa. Sierra Leone and other unfortunate nations were depleted, sucked out. Processing rutile, a gray, pock-marked mineral, to extract titanium dioxide caused the usual environmental embarrassments: the flooding of lowlands, deforestation, tailings like bedsores on the terrain—nothing new, nothing shocking. NASA needed new sources of titanium, chromium, gold, platinum, silver, and other rare metals—especially as space colonization became practical. NASA's mining component had set up a space colony on Arabia Terra, a Martian wasteland—blighted by erosion not caused by humans but by water, spewed out by volcanoes about three million years prior. This underground water was now eagerly, wastefully, pumped out by the colonists.

Troy, our Martian hero, felt extracting metals was worth the human costs. Look at titanium—it had strengthened the Mars rover's suspension system in 2009. And for that, Troy was thankful. If it weren't for the Mars rover finding water, he wouldn't be on Mars now, in a Laundromat, with a steady job. Troy believed in progress.

When the pain subsided, Troy braced himself on a machine and stood. None of the miners paid much notice; one was grinding against a machine, watching the spin cycle. Bobbi unlocked the office door and called him to come with her. Inside, stacks of Chinese takeout containers and fast food bags filled a metal trashcan. A clipboard on the wall listed customer names that corresponded to amounts refunded for broken machines.

Troy still wanted to touch Bobbi. He wanted to unbutton her top and let the neck breathe. She was in her sixties, a black woman from Texas, whose husband used to sign up for all the free gifts on the credit card bills. She'd told him they weren't free—nothing was—but he wouldn't believe her. They came to Mars to make a killing on the Laundromat, but her husband died at a Martian bar; he went for a free lap dance and got asphyxiated by a stripper with one eye. Troy picked up a pair of pliers, wire cutters, and a roll of wire.

"Don't talk to nobody," she said. "Stay out of

trouble." Troy nodded, holding his hands by his side. By dryer fourteen, he cut and wove pieces of wire into a tight mesh, sealing the air vent, wishing he could tighten the wire around a drug addict's throat. They were everywhere on the ship, like fruit flies.

A faded cardboard sign above the wall of dryers read: RESPECT YOUR NEIGHBORHOOD. He saw a girl in her early twenties, smoking a cigarette near the corridor. He felt love. He set the tools on the dryer and finished the cola, so his breath would smell sugary, as if to impart his goodness. Cool jazz from the corner speakers couldn't soothe Troy's fever.

The girl met his standards, which got higher every year. Not that he'd try anything, of course, but what she did and how she looked and how her dirty laundry got that way were matters to discuss. His place.

Troy knew he frightened people; he had bad posture and his teeth were graying. He often wore extra-large from the lost-and-found box, with someone else's stains. Sometimes he wore rainbow suspenders.

If he could work up the nerve, he'd say, "Let's meet tonight. I'll tell you my secrets. Like this one: Every night I can't swallow right. I clutch my stomach before sleep, kneading into the sore spot beneath my belly button. Evil beings bowl in my guts and slam pins against the walls."

He had guilt. When Troy was young, he spied on his sister. One day he hid in the media closet behind an accordion door, watching Guineveve stare at the TV in their living room den. Marvin the cartoon

Martian told the space dog to get that Earth creature. The drum rolled. Troy didn't know what Marvin meant by a uranium PU-36 explosive space modulator, but he liked it when Martin said, "Isn't that wonderful? Now we can blow up the Earth!" The trombones on the soundtrack slid, and the xylophone went berserk.

Their mother came into the room. She grabbed Guineveve's arm, pulling her out from under a blanket. Her mother had to bring her to the cheap doctor, the one at the mall. She was always taking them to doctors. That's why Troy liked to hide.

Troy opened the door and threw a ball without thinking. It arced above the teddy bears lining the shelves. It hit a glass vase, which shattered, and pieces landed on Guineveve's face and dress. Their mother held her to her shoulder. Guineveve's pain became a warm oval of spit, mucus, and tears on her mother's dress. When she leaned back to scream, her face glittered with red dots of blood and glass. Or maybe that memory was false? Maybe she got covered in blood when she stood behind a pane of glass and he kicked, kung-fu-style. Little kids who broke glass got spanked. So did little kids who drew pictures on the dryers with permanent markers. Whipped around by their mother, with her death grip on their noodle arms. Each time Troy pressed the red button, he hoped the rays would kill his Earth memories, false or real.

A pair of boots and a sleeping bag thudded inside dryer number eight. Troy huffed on his glasses. He lifted the lid to washer number five. A sock looked as if it had strangled itself around the agitator. He picked it up and put it into the girl's dryer, number seven.

The smoking girl wore silver Mylar leggings and rhinestone flip-flops. Troy named her Susie. Her barrette held her bangs aloft, like a hedge he wanted to trim. She shivered in her leopard-print coat, something she got, no doubt, from screwing one of the roaming flea-market scabs who visited the space colony every fortnight. She stamped out a cigarette and kicked it into the corridor in a fluid movement.

"Nice aim," Troy said. He pointed to a book on the folding table, next to a stack of Jehovah's Witness pamphlets. "What are you understanding?"

"You want the red?" Susie asked.

"I'm sorry, but what are you understanding? I've taken a lot of computer classes. And the books I used were all titled *Understanding This, Understanding That.*"

"It's *Undertaker*. Excuse me." She picked up her book and got a cart. He wandered to the bulletin board, as if they'd never spoken. But he felt that weird energy of connection, as if his heart were overheating just for her.

When Susie emptied the clothes from the dryer into the cart, Troy saw an opportunity. He got one edged with gray duct tape and blocked Susie's cart with his, trapping her in the narrow aisle.

She looked down and scratched her cheek.

"I like gross things," Troy said to her. "Your scab

is not gross to me."

She laughed. "Do you like medical textbooks?"

"No. That's too gross." Troy thought, Why is she asking me? What can she guess?

"Do you like dead animals?"

"Not particularly. I like the precipice of grossness, like hearing a gross story and being able to back away."

Bobbi rustled her bag of food. "Settle down now, Troy," she said.

If he could get Susie to look him in the eyes for ten minutes, they would fall in love. Troy had fallen for much less.

He reached across his cart and picked up the blue sock he had put in Susie's dryer. "This is mine, perhaps?" he asked.

"What the hell," she said. "Don't put your laundry in with mine!"

"Oh, so sorry. I'm sure you didn't have room to dry one little sock? I'll pay you back the extra quarter."

"Get away," she said. She picked up the sock with two fingers and flung it at him. He smiled, touched. She looked as if she might cry, but she coughed instead, a hacking that led to dry heaves. She leaned against a dryer and wiped her eyes.

Bobbi stood and pulled the TV earplugs out. "Troy, take it easy and everything will be fine."

She's jealous, Troy thought. Just the other day she had told him about her cancer treatment. She had her hair up in netting and wore a hospital gown, and he told her she looked great. He of all people should know. He made it his business to study women.

Where did Bobbi get off, with her fears that Troy would bother the customers? He stuffed the sock and a couple of damp towels from the lost-and-found box into a plastic trash bag.

He studied the bulletin board again as if that were the reason he'd come in. A flyer read: ENLARGE YOUR MIND. FIRST SESSION FREE. CONTACT DR. MARCY GRABLE, REGISTERED THERAPIST. He thought of telling Susie, "Hey, there's the word *rapist* in the word *therapist*. A coincidence?" Instead, he ripped down the flyer and walked out.

At home, Troy narrated his life as if to a lawyer, guilty as charged: Here I am: a fat man on his toilet with a chipped wooden seat. Everything's filtered with a gold light. Piles of computer magazines are tipped against the hamper, and my bare feet rest on a plush rug. A soft cascade of speckled vomit runs across the ceiling and down the shower curtain, as if it were a map of the Dark Continent. I have chromium poisoning. I keep it a secret. I vomit only at home. Peeking out of the linen closet is a pink shoe, a mule, with feathers.

You want to see me. You want to, and here I am. Cramping and aching.

He went to the kitchenette and fried baloney on the plug-in stovetop unit, spattering butter on his shirt. Eating his baloney sandwich, he looked out the bulletproof window to the Laundromat across the corridor. He figured Susie would come back eventually. He liked his job. He liked where he lived. So easy to fit in here. His heart pounded when he finally spotted her, now wearing a red raincoat as if she wanted him to be the Woodsman, saving her from the Wolf. He put down the rest of his sandwich, locked the door, and walked into the Laundromat. He smelled his fingers. He couldn't help it. He wished he'd eaten honey instead.

Troy clutched his lucky pebble in his fist. Bobbi was gone for the night, but a few customers—old miners—folded their vomit-stained clothes or read newspapers. The buzz of fluorescent lights crawled through Troy's brain. Susie ducked her head when she saw him. Perhaps she is shy.

"Susie!" he said—but that wasn't even her real name. How would he learn it?

She turned around. She had a screwdriver in her hand. The little thief. His precious girl.

She handed the screwdriver to Troy. Did her slender fingers graze his on purpose, with her rings so fragile, with her shimmery silver nails?

"Help me, will you?" she said. Her voice was slurred.

He took the screwdriver and wondered what to do with it. Should he stick it in his eye, like Oedipus did to his own bloodshot orbs with two pins from his mother's dress? Or no, something simpler, She probably wanted money. He banged it against the coin-op machine. The boxes of laundry flakes shook inside.

"Try again," she said. "I don't feel well. Stick it up the other way." She winked, but her upper fake eyelash got stuck on her lower lid.

He jammed the screwdriver into the change slot. He moved it around, feeling for the lever to open the valve. He sweated, shaking coins loose that clattered on the ground. He couldn't concentrate; he was so filled with longing. He couldn't let the scream out. He could feel it in his throat.

Susie knelt down, under her red cape, and picked up the coins. She left with a quick wave. The bandit. She didn't say good-bye. It wasn't because of him—it was the fault of the drug addict who came in while she was on the floor.

The drug addict, a thin white guy with a sore on his lip, shook a stack of religious pamphlets in the air. He lurched toward Troy. He spoke loudly, his breath tainted by sour vomit. "Got any money for old age disease?"

Troy's shirt smelled like greasy meat. He felt ashamed. He walked out to the corridor, calling over and over, "I love you, Susie!" But she was gone.

The next morning, Troy took a handful of quarters he'd found under dryers and hired a motorcycle driver, the least sick one he could find. The weather was cold and clear. His appointment was at noon. He wore his space suit, duct-taped from all the damage incurred by dust storms. He coughed into his respirator and handed the driver the address. He loved being outdoors, feeling one-tenth his Earth mass, but the air was carcinogenic, and the respirators were notoriously faulty.

The motorbike wove between triple-decker buses with huge, chained wheels, taking miners to work, the windows caked with dried vomit and dust; water hawkers with weights around their waists hung upside-down from the roofs, handing water bottles to the parched workers inside. Troy's driver paused to let a convoy pass. Troy said a prayer to the Tikonravev Crater, which once held an ancient lake. Today, no clouds of dry ice obscured Troy's vision of it, a huge pedestal crater perched above the land. Martians worshipped it, collecting rocks to caress like magnetized statues of saints.

This sector mined titanium to treat sewage and toxic waste; NASA shipped it to outposts past the asteroid belt. Suction pipes dredged miles of Martian soil; like impervious worms they separated the heavy minerals from the worthless sands, moving slowly through the terrain and shitting out unneeded dirt into the drilling holes.

Troy's driver parked in front of Dr. Grable's office, enclosed by a gate topped with concertina wire and security cameras. Troy pressed a door buzzer and was let in to a heated, blue room. It had high windows and a cow's skull on the wall.

The doctor was spindly, but her wrinkles looked severe. She held out her hand, smooth, with no discolorations. Troy put his palms behind his back and shook his head no. "It's OK, Troy," she said. "There's no red button here. I hope it's OK I call you by your first name."

Troy told her he didn't have a lot of money. He came here because it was free. Dr. Grable shushed him, calming him. She sat at the edge of a couch and rubbed the cushion in a circular pattern, motioning Troy to sit by her. "I met this man the other day," she said. She looked at Troy, not blinking. He tried not to blink, either. "I told him to see someone in the healing profession," she said. "I gave him my card and patted him on the shoulder. I knew no one had touched him in a while. How do you feel about that?"

She tried to pat him on the leg, but he moved away, his stomach churning. He was so thirsty. The purple cushions on the couch smelled odd, like shampooed goats.

Dr. Grable left the room, saying she would bring him something special. He looked for the indent on the couch from her thighs and ass. He was alone with the cow's skull and its empty sockets. A rhythm of light pulsed from the bulb above his head, yellow and blue like pictures of a sunny sky in a children's book, but loud chirps pierced from somewhere in the building, like a smoke alarm with dead batteries, but they didn't have smoke alarms on Mars. He was worried. Why wouldn't anyone stop it?

Dr. Grable returned, smiling with greasy teeth and lips, and handed him a stack of postcards. He studied one from Peru, of mummies in loose wrappings, whose skulls didn't betray one happy thought.

"You don't believe I was ever young," he said. The air was strange in here, making him confused, making him feel high and paranoid. "That's why you handed me these images of dead things. You mock me."

"Troy, I don't judge you," Dr. Grable said.

"Do you remember the alphabet on the walls? The girls clapping about Miss Mary Mack all dressed in black? And the hermit crab. They forgot to water it, or they didn't want to. They wanted the water for themselves. It died in its glass prison, shrunken and inert."

He hoped he didn't have to leave yet. He hoped she wouldn't rush outside to the driver, to tell him how Troy disgusted her, to touch him instead. The doctor walked across the room to look out the window. Every so often she tapped it, as if in beat with the mining equipment.

"You think you know me," he said. He sat up, and his voice got louder and more insistent. "And when you're done talking, I'll still be the kid who stands on the chair when the teacher goes out of the room. All the kids look up at me. There's Sandy in red boots and Laura in gray tights. I have their attention. I press out my stomach and pull my shirt up. I'm eight, just like the rest."

He crossed the room to the doctor and put his finger on her forehead. She pushed it away.

"The kids tease me about my name, Troy Carter," he said. "They sing: 'Toilet Farter, Toilet Farter,' and I chant along. I'll do anything for them."

He pressed her forehead again. "Do you understand?" he asked. She pulled down his hand and twisted his wrist between her thumb and middle finger, pressing on a nerve. He dropped to his knees. She squeezed harder and her voice got deeper.

"I don't need a red button here," she said. She let go, and he tried not to faint. He had touched the red button so often, though, that his animal brain, the thalamus, had gotten stronger.

"My father died recently," she said. "We didn't get along. I hope it's OK to share. I like to be open with my patients when I think it can be therapeutic."

"Your dad. Your poor dad!" Troy wanted to cry, but his tear ducts were dried out. "I wish I had a dad."

The doctor told him to lie down on the concrete floor. She reached for a box from a shelf and put on a ribbed latex glove. Troy lay on his back, clothed and quivering.

"This won't hurt," she said. She stuck her hand in his mouth and pulled his cheek outward.

"No," he moaned. He wanted the chirps from the smoke alarm to stop. He tried to relax, but her fingers felt like crabs. He resisted the urge to bite. She must have sensed his discomfort. She smiled and took her hand out.

"Anything you'd like to say?"

"I'm punching a hole in the wall, and the water is seeping down and out across the top of the window, as if by magic, and dripping into a series of plastic cups. And I know there's something clawing inside my throat."

"Yes, Troy. Something is inside you. A pigeon's claw."

"A pigeon's claw. A wolverine's claw. Something just stuck. Can I get some water? I'm so thirsty all the time. I try praying. Nothing helps."

"First a hug."

They embraced, kneeling awkwardly on the floor. Troy felt light-headed. He focused on the jingling of her silver bangles. He closed his eyes and breathed in her soft, ribbed sweater and thick bra strap. He opened his eyes and saw dandruff on Dr. Grable's shoulder. The flakes made her seem so human, so vulnerable.

"How did he die?" Troy stammered.

"Let me get you some water," she said. She walked over to a pitcher on a table.

Troy sat up. He noticed she didn't move right. She walked steadily, with no adjustments for the thin air. It felt different in here. More buoyant. The air smelled bad. It was making him sick.

"My dad was doing germ warfare in the garden when he died," she said. "He had a heart attack." She handed Troy a glass of water. He swirled it, and sediment rose from the bottom.

"Remember, we weren't close," she said. "He was poisoning the caterpillars."

"It's bad to kill," Troy whispered.

"They were eating the broccoli," she said.

She knelt by him, getting ready to put her hand in his mouth again. Maybe she was an android. Why would a normal woman touch him? He hated androids. They ruined everything for the lovers on Mars. He took her hand, cold under the latex glove.

"You said I could touch you?" he asked.

"How do you feel?" she asked.

He bit her hand, ripping the latex through to the skin and spitting out pieces of flesh. The skin tasted like a rubber band, lightly scented with baby powder. He gagged. But if he ate her synthetic skin, maybe it would calm his stomach. Like a poison ivy cure, eating what harms him to build immunity. She slapped him across the face, which was part of her programming.

The doctor looked on the floor for the skin, which wriggled and glistened. Troy stepped on her hand. The android could focus only on her skin. She couldn't fight back. Under the skin, was a titanium core, laced with glowing wires. Troy didn't have much time, but there was so much skin to eat. But it tasted so bad. He was afraid he'd vomit again. Her skeleton was as shiny as the coins refunded to Laundromat customers.

Troy squatted down, his knees cracking. He picked up a piece of skin and dangled it in front of her.

"I know why Laundromats and your office are blue," he said. "Orange and red make you want to leave—like the orange walls of lice-removal stations or fast-food joints. Blue makes customers want to stay and add more quarters. You want me to come back. You never want me to get well."

"Bad, bad Troy," she said. "Toilet Farter." Her voice crackled. He stood up and got the cow's skull. While the doctor rocked back and forth, making twittering sounds, he hit her face with the skull. Her eyeball popped into the machinery inside.

Troy made sure his lucky pebble was still in his pocket. He said a prayer to the rock spirits, thanking them. He paid attention so even the worst moments on Mars made sense, so when he finally sacrificed himself in the crater, he would have something worthwhile for which to atone.

SENTIENT TIMES

Evidently the cat shat behind the couch. Or was that word *evidently* somewhat absurd, adding a frisson of snobbery to a crass act, or was shitting less crass if a cat did it? What if worms were involved? Or if dried shit had to be cut from the cat's tail? And if the cat were ill, did this story suddenly veer to sentimentality?

She was getting divorced. All marriage vows were lies.

The husband painted with She-Artist and her boyfriend, He-Artist, for three days in the basement, during which She-Artist and He-Artist held their hands in buckets of cold water. The ultimate ménage à trois.

The wife cried around her husband like she was a baby. The husband told her she dampened his creativity. She didn't value his soul.

"Was marriage hard?" she asked.

"It's hard to exist," he said.

She talked to her mom. Her mom said, "Sometimes I think, where has my life gone?"

She comforted her son. Her son said, "I like to munch and pee."

THE SHREW OF D.C.

M. waited until the answering machine picked up. The light blinked and she dared him to speak. She touched her toes on the rental-beige carpet, and when she stood up, she picked up the receiver. "Hey, babe," he said.

He told her it took the shrew longer to find the clothes hamper when she drank. That's what he brought up, right away, even though they could be recounting their rendezvous in the private hallway—the one with the eagles embossed in gold above the doors. He said the shrew had thrashed around their private rooms just now and forgot that she had a maid. Her dry-cleaning pile—her worsted green suits—made her irate. The press corps made fun of her clothes, especially that bitch from *The New York Times*. His wife looked at the size of her skirts and wanted to slice hunks from her ass. M. could tell he said that part cautiously. He knew she didn't like her ass, either. Since she was his mistress, he had to be tender about that part of her anatomy.

She put her happiness in something external and unreliable—the big glub of him.

"She found out you bought that ficus. She put it out on the patio and it died," he said. "Oops, hold on a minute, babe."

M. wrote *balls* on her hand when he put her on hold. She licked it off.

She didn't tell him that the ficus was called the weeping fig. If she'd told him, he'd think she was referring to herself, whom he called Ms. Weepy-Woo, when she wasn't breathing heavily, pretending to orgasm. He said all the women he'd been with were loud, so why was she so quiet?

Everyone figured she was stupid and truly believed he'd leave the shrew for her. Mostly, he liked to inform her, via her vagina, or her mouth, or her tits under the Calvin Klein bra, of the times he'd been with others, because she triggered all of them.

He wouldn't stop talking even when he was pressed against her; that afternoon she'd seen a trail of dust that the housekeepers missed in the hallway. He had one hand holding her head down and the other on his private phone, talking to the prime minister of Ireland. That nosy bitch secretary knocked. "Sorry, babe. You know, I love you, honey," he said, and shuttled her out the door.

Now, while on hold, she looked down at her dress, the one she could barely afford to have dry-cleaned, at the splotches of dried cum. His sperm tasted like a mouth full of buttermilk and heat, and she often kept it in her mouth and pressed her tongue against it. She tried to taste the spot on her dress, but her finger tasted of salty chips. She hung up the phone without saying goodnight, took off the dress, and placed it in the back of her closet, just in case.

THE SCORPION

A rusted Ford Falcon eased into the parking lot from the access road. It hailed from the 1960s: a two-door sedan with dog-dish hubcaps. Barb remembered them. She liked the Falcon's taillights; they looked like wanton tits. Caked-on bugs obscured the license plate, and the chrome bumper sagged. Even the turn signal blinked at half-speed.

Barb sat outside the motel office under a mildewed patio umbrella. She couldn't open it all the way, so it listed to the right. She dotted her nails with yellow polish. She was trying to redo the daisies painted at the salon down the highway. The polish had gotten chipped last night. Her painted dots blurred into the yellow, like a broken egg. Barb imagined her mother saying, "Make sure your cuticles are trimmed and your nails look pretty, so your boyfriend knows you care." She doused a cotton ball in nail polish remover and wiped off the mess. The odor stung like a line of speed.

Barb fanned herself with a local casino brochure.

She pretended not to notice the car headed toward her. Ants scrambled over the dirt and weeds by Barb's feet, and the heat seared her toes. Normally she'd be inside the office, with the AC, but not today. Too depressing. She adjusted her butt in the plastic chair.

A rubber ball lay in the grass. She should put it in the lost-and-found box, but the kid who owned it, a girl with a runny nose and a Malibu Beach Bum t-shirt, was long gone. Indian gambling was about the only thing happening on this side of Clear Lake, California, besides hot springs and pot farms on government land.

The Falcon parked next to Barb. She took a sip of water and wiped her mouth. She pulled a scab from the underside of her wrist. It exposed raw skin that pulsed in the heat. The driver rolled down the window and smiled. His tongue poked out between his tobacco-stained teeth.

Barb squinted behind her sunglasses. The guy could be in his late thirties, about Jake's age. His lank blond hair hung behind his ears. He picked a flake of tobacco off his tongue and flicked it out the window, as if he were dismissing her. But she hadn't done anything. Not to him. To Jake, true, but it wasn't her fault. She stood up and adjusted her terry-cloth shorts. Her thighs were crosshatched with grooves from the chair. On one leg, the lines covered a bruise.

"Need a room?" she asked.

"I'm looking for Jake," the man said. "I'm Terrence—an old friend." He got out of the car. He was holding a deflated duffel bag. His thin cotton shirt was frayed at the collar, and he wore brown old-man pants. He coughed and cleared his throat.

"Hot enough?" she asked.

"When's he coming back?"

"I haven't seen him. Maybe he's at the casino or with his ex-wife." Barb kept her voice flat, but approachable. Her leg quivered, so she jammed her hand on it to get control. Her mom had claimed she'd craved dog biscuits when she was pregnant; she'd even eaten some. Maybe that's why Barb turned out strange.

She wiped her forehead. Yesterday Jake had sat across from her. He was tall with a dirty tan. He sucked the pulp out of a mango and licked his upper lip. Fidgeting, he tossed the green peel on the gravel for Barb to pick up later, after they fucked for the last time.

Jake yelled at her—as if he were here now—to pay attention. To not screw up. Terrence was an opportunity, like she'd read about in self-help books people left in the rooms. Maybe he had something to do with Jake's drug deals, but those guys had code names. She couldn't guess by looking if Terrence was "Squirrel," "Grapehead," or "Dead Guy."

"You look like a smart girl," Terrence said. "Jake owes me money, but it's nothing we can't work out."

The phone rang inside the office. "Maybe that's him," Terrence said. He walked toward the office door. Barb shoved her chair back and it toppled over. She hurried after him, brushing against a saguaro cactus. A flower, white and gooey, bloomed from its side.

The office rug shimmered with broken glass and bits of plastic gravel from a smashed aquarium. A few black snails clustered on the damp shards. The jigsaw puzzles Barb had planned on gluing together lay on the rug. She didn't have the heart to throw them out.

Terrence gave the phone to Barb without saying anything. She watched Terrence, only half-listening to Gloria—the only other guest, if her pain-in-the-ass sister could be called a guest—berating her on the line. Terrence paced the room. He opened desk drawers and looked on the bookshelves. "There must be a pack around here," he said. "You and me, we'll get a game going. What do you play? Poker? Crazy Eights? We should do something fun till Jake gets back."

A couple of nights ago, Jake had chased Barb around the desk and pulled her down behind it, not caring that her knees banged against the legs of the metal chair. He took out his Leatherman knife from his pocket and poked the blade through her shirt until it pressed against her nipple. "Don't flinch," he said.

Now, with the phone cradled between her neck and shoulder, she sniffed her shirt. It smelled like Jake—like motor oil and dusty leather. She believed him when he said she was beautiful. She missed his stuffy weight on her.

Barb sat on the desk, jiggling her leg. She had a clear path to the door. If she could only get the keys to the Falcon. Maybe she could play strip poker for the keys. Get her sister in on it.

Terrence picked up the coffee carafe that held

rescued fish. Black mollies swam in murky laps. "What's going on?" he asked. Without waiting for her to answer, he opened a blind and punched a button on the AC unit. The machine sputtered to life, spewing cigarette smoke and a chilly whine. He found a pack of cards and tossed an ace on the floor.

"Who's that?" Gloria said to Barb on the phone. "Who drove in?"

"I'm helping a guest," Barb said to her.

"But there's a scorpion in the bathroom sink!" Gloria said.

"I'll help you with the goddamn scorpion," Barb said.

She cupped her hand over the mouthpiece. "Sorry for the mess," she said to Terrence.

"Some party," Terrence said. He flicked a queen at her. "Does Jake cheat at cards? Yeah, he cheats," he said, looking at Barb's face. "You like cheaters?"

Barb got a key from a hook on the wall. "Here's your room key. Your room's by your car. Checkout's at noon. Since you're Jake's friend, it's on us."

"I'm going to take a look around," Terrence said. "Don't go anywhere I can't find you."

After Terrence left, Barb picked up a splintered baseball bat from behind the desk. She wrapped a white guest towel around it. She didn't want to alarm Gloria.

Barb headed up the iron staircase. Sweat soaked through the crotch of her shorts. She tried to wave it dry. A line of sweat ran down the front of her shirt, settling under her bra.

Her foot caught on a torn piece of green AstroTurf, and she clutched the metal railing. “Shit,” she said. She looked down at the pool and shook her head at a blue tube top floating on the surface. Makes the place look trashy, she thought.

She reached the landing and wasn’t surprised to see Terrence, smoking and carrying a bucket of ice. “I thought you’d need my help,” he said.

He must have gone up the back way. She wondered what Jake would make of Terrence. Was he a threat or a pansy-assed gangster poseur?

Beige drapes covered the windows of her sister’s room. Barb knocked on the door, though it was cracked open. She stepped inside, avoiding the bed sheets wadded on the floor. Terrence followed her.

Gloria beckoned them to the bathroom door. She had thick red lips and round cheeks. Her eyeliner raced under her eyelids to meet the half-moon of blue eye shadow from above. Her large tits were squished into a low top. She looked sleazy, but Barb didn’t say anything.

Barb blinked and took off her sunglasses. She saw Gloria’s lips moving, but couldn’t focus on the words. She rolled the bat in her hand and forced herself to cross the room.

The heavy bat and the steam from the shower shrunk the bathroom. The faucet dripped in the stained sink basin. A towel, rusty at the edges, hung on a hook. When Terrence squeezed Barb’s shoulder, she brushed him off. Ass.

“It bit me after I got out of the shower,” Gloria

said. She held up a swollen finger. "My armpit hurts, too. I think my blood is poisoned."

"Let me see your finger," Terrence said. He dropped his cigarette and moved Gloria under the bathroom light. "It could be a sting. You can't usually see the entry wound. Sometimes scorpions bite when they mate."

"Thank God you arrived." Gloria smiled at him and leaned forward, as if she'd fall into him. He dripped ice onto her fingers and palm.

The scorpion hunkered in the sink. It was about the size of Barb's thumb, and its body was golden, like a piece of sap.

"What are you waiting for? Kill it!" Gloria said.

"Go bionic on the bitch," Terrence said, laughing.

Barb slammed the tip of the bat against the scorpion. Its guts oozed milky yellow, forming a crescent that echoed the shape of its crushed body.

That evening, Terrence and Barb became drinking buddies. They sat on the patio by the Falcon with bags of ice cooling their feet. "It's a hot day. And that's a leather seat, and I got a thin skirt," Barb recited.

Terrence asked, "Where'd you hear that from?"

"*The Postman Always Rings Twice.* The original." Barb sipped her special scotch, which erupted in her mouth like smoke. The bottle came in a cardboard box printed with a map of Scotland. It made her feel well traveled. She used to drink with her mother; that's how they got along best. Her mother had cooked meatloaf every time a new man came into their lives. One time she wore a new silk blouse, and the new man, who had red, splotchy skin, pulled her to him, stretching the blouse tight in the back and bunching it into a ball. Her mother turned up Willie Nelson on the radio and kissed this man with her tongue. The spices popped and exploded, and the ground beef charred in the pan.

Barb liked her scotch with ice and lemon. Terrence took a splash of Coke with his. "May I?" she asked, tipping the bottle toward him. She actually felt okay, maybe even human, but not exactly feminine. She tightened her bra strap and chewed on an egg salad sandwich from the office fridge. She pressed the soft yolk against her teeth. "My mom told me, 'I bet you'll end up knowing a lot about scotch before you die.' What a thing to say to your daughter, huh?"

He cheered her on to drink more. "So why didn't Jake call?" he asked.

"This place is a dump. He's selling it. He doesn't care about us. He never has." Barb swirled the scotch around the plastic cup. She needed to see Jake's body, but her brain wanted more alcohol swimming around in it.

"I bet I could turn it around—once I get paid." He tipped his glass toward Gloria's room. "Think your sister will join us?"

"She likes to sleep a lot."

"Are you sure you don't have more ideas about Jake somewhere in those curls?" he asked.

"I can still play cards with you if you want," Barb said.

Terrence tore open a package of Good & Plenty candy and put a handful of licorice in his mouth. Barb looked up the stairs, hoping Gloria would find something to watch on TV. Instead, she saw Gloria walking down slowly, gripping the handrail.

Gloria walked to the table and opened her palm. She dumped out a handful of quartz pebbles collected by the creek. She stuck each one in a hole in the table. Some fell through and some stayed suspended. "Where's my scotch, honey?" she asked Terrence. He dipped his finger in his drink for her.

"I'll get another bottle," Barb said. She stood and swayed, jiggling her hips. She had to check Jake's room. She unlocked his bedroom by the office and turned on the light. Jake's blood and piss formed a misshapen angel on the rug. His body looked purplish-red. Barb squeezed her stomach under her shirt and tried to think. She leaned down and put her hand on the back of his neck. Falling to her knees, she held the edge of the comforter, whispering half-words and moaning. One time in the woods, by his property, he'd put a piece of sap on her tongue. It turned rancid in her mouth and she spat it into the creek. How she wished for that sap now, or anything he could give her.

The door opened and Gloria and Terrence walked in.

"I didn't mean it," Barb said. "I didn't know what to do with him all day. What could I do?"

Gloria walked to the TV, bolted to a small table. She turned on a nature show and kept her finger pressed on the remote's volume button until the green volume bars crossed the screen. The narrator droned on about the mating habits of tarantulas. Gloria placed the remote on the TV, next to cans of Tecate and Sprite. She crouched behind the TV set, wiping the rug with the corner of her shirt. "The ants are going to come in," Gloria said. "You guys spilled the soda. You didn't clean it up. Why didn't you at least put a towel down?"

"Gloria, honey. Look what's happening," Barb said. "Jake's gone." She wiped her bloody hand across her shirt.

"What the hell are you thinking?" Terrence said to Barb. He knelt down next to Jake's body. "Why didn't you tell me earlier, you idiot?" He smacked Barb in the mouth. She put her hand to it to stop the pain, but refused to cry.

Gloria rubbed Jake's hair. "How could you do this?" she asked Barb softly. "Why are you such a monster?"

Barb pushed Gloria back. "He's mine," she said.

Terrence stood and looked at his watch. "We need to think," he said. "I need his pot plants. Tell me where he's growing them. Don't bullshit me." Terrence spoke in a deadpan voice, as if he dealt with dead bodies all the time, but Barb saw his hands shake. He lit a cigarette to disguise his panic.

"I can take you there," Barb said. "But what about him?" She pointed to Jake.

"He'll come with us," Terrence said. Barb pulled the flowered bedspread off the mattress and wrapped Jake's body in it, as if he were her doll. She looked at the headboard she used to grip. Reaching her arms under Jake's torso, Barb asked Gloria for help. Terrence picked up his legs but Barb said, "No. Gloria's got to do it."

On the TV, a man in a blazer and jeans pushed a woman in a garden swing. She pumped her legs and threw her head back so her neck made a smooth curve. Her laugh boomed out of the speakers until Terrence pulled the cord from the outlet.

Gloria and Barb half-dragged, half-carried the body to the Falcon and laid it in the trunk. The moon, almost full, was held in place by swaying, gray-green clouds.

A few miles from the motel, Barb told Terrence to turn down a dirt road. He swore, saying he almost missed it, the woods were so dark. The Falcon rattled in and out of potholes that looked like ink soup. Barb sat with Gloria in the front seat, with Gloria half on her lap, comatose, her cheek pressed against the window. Barb didn't want to be in the back, with only a bit of stained vinyl, foam, and coiled springs separating her from Jake.

Clouds of dust boiled under the car. A truck coming toward them flashed its lights. Barb reached across Terrence and turned the headlights on and off.

Terrence pulled down the door of the glove compartment. "Get me another pack of cigs. Do you fucking want us to get caught?"

"It's what we do to be friendly. It's called being local," Barb said.

She told Terrence to turn off the road by a large iron

gate. Barb got out of the car, entered the combination on the lock, and swung the gate forward to let the car through. Terrence parked by a stand of oaks. Barb could run, but where? She walked to the car and stood by Gloria. She could be strong. Terrence took out the duffel bag and a flashlight. He lit a cigarette and lugged Jake out of the trunk. Gloria and Barb held each other.

"I'd better not get a tick bite," Gloria said.

They hiked in the darkness past spindly manzanita trees and tall ghost pines that swayed and whistled. When Barb's arms ached from carrying Jake's torso, she switched with Gloria, swapping for the bottle of scotch. Terrence held Jake's legs, not wavering when crossing fallen limbs or moss-covered rocks. The heat eased, and Barb listened for the frogs' mating calls and the creek to guide her. They trudged past hills blackened by fire, near a ridge that glowed red from a geothermal heat mine.

On a hill above the creek, Barb pointed out indentations in the land, like small altars. In each one grew marijuana plants fed by black irrigation pipes. Terrence and Barb laid Jake under a ghost pine, covering him with the bloodstained motel comforter. Terrence said he would look as if a thief had killed him.

Barb opened the flap to Jake's tent. She stepped over eggshells, beer bottles, and a porn magazine. She moved a shovel near the tent opening and brought out a tin box of matches.

Terrence filled the duffel bag with the plants, carefully preserving the roots. He stooped over, scooping with his hand and the end of the flashlight.

She lit a match to help him see, but he motioned her away. He looked more goblin than man.

Gloria paced in the dirt, shivering. "I want to get out of here," she said.

Barb considered the shovel in the tent. One good whack and she'd have the car with Gloria. Two good whacks...she looked at Jake for a sign, but Gloria had covered his face with twigs and leaves, and Barb was too spooked to pull them off.

She frowned. Last night, after feeding the fish, Barb had left the office to get some ice. Jake had Gloria hiked up against the machine so she had nowhere to fall but down on his cock. They didn't see her—or pretended not to. She waited until Gloria scurried to her room to take her pills. In the office, Barb concentrated on a Springbok puzzle till Jake came to find her. She had to hold one hand with the other, it was shaking so badly. "Help me look for a piece," she said. She swung the baseball bat at him and smashed the aquarium. He knocked over her puzzles, and she chased him into his room. It went further than she had wanted. She swung at him, but that didn't kill him. He hit his head on the TV. Who would believe her? You don't die from TVs; you die from wooden bats. *Blunt force trauma*—she learned the damn term from TV.

She clutched her stomach and sat across from Jake's body in the woods, wishing they could trade places. Everyone wondered why her mother went crazy, worrying after Barb and the bad men she dated. And now Barb had to worry about her sister. With the duffel bag full, Gloria hung on Terrence's arm and shuffled her feet in the dirt, begging him to feel for ticks on her neck and waist.

Terrence zipped up the bag and pointed the flashlight in Barb's eyes. "Ready?" he asked.

"I need to take a piss." She lit a match by a rock covered with green lichen and pulled down her shorts. The pee spattered on orange mushrooms, like drops of blood.

HOSPITAL VISIT

You're lying on a bed. You're waiting to have eggs removed forcibly for in vitro fertilization. The people next to you are loud. They're behind a curtain but you can hear them clearly. You're trying to relax because a nurse has jammed an IV in your hand. It's painful. But you want to make a baby.

The woman next to you is a patient but also a hospital orderly. "I saw an elderly person whose eye had exploded," she says to the nurse. "She had glaucoma and high blood pressure."

The nurse says, "I hope you don't have to see that again."

That lady tells more stories. "One time a patient died on a plastic air bag bed. The bed collapsed and the housekeeper didn't know it. She took the bed to get sterilized and no one could find the body."

Quiet. Nothing's quiet here. You are part of a death home. Beeping machines, cold air, naked bodies under thin gowns, thin sheets.

THE DESPERATE ONES

(Lower Haight and South of Market, San Francisco, 1990s)

I.

I'm tired of this neighborhood. The intersection of Haight and Steiner—my world and a little part of Charles's.

Right now I am high. He is watching TV like a sucker. I want to sock him in the spine. "Pay some attention to me." I have enough salt to cure the wound afterwards. I am so bored.

I am going to get picked up by some dovetailed orphan. He can set me against his sickness. I'll castrate the sucker and walk out into the sunlight, lightheaded, and happy—and then I'll vomit in Safeway. Yes, I'll do that.

Call my sister a "nice girl"—well shit on you.

Listen, Charles, you don't need to buy anything. You have me. And I am everything for you. I will rip out the eyes of that product that takes your interest from me. I see you through the glass.

You read so intently the liner notes of that worthless LP. Sand in your eyes. Put that damn record down. Take me to the garden. And prop up the moon. If we don't repeat. You really have my tongue. Forever. And I can keep your words where they will gain interest.

II.

The reason why I'm not here not wanted by anyone not given ample amounts of "sugar" not even a back-rub. Know when I really need you to help out look how I get done my money my dope my time are things I don't give up to anyone you gotten all three I have gotten attacked arguments downright ABUSIVE mentally. I can't hang no more. Sorry wish it was different to work ALL day so I can be home for you just to have you shoot my dope and split. Well baby I'm not a jerk or a treat I'm a person.

III.

DEAR~~EST~~ MOTHER; IT IS WITH SINCEREST APOLOGIES, FOR THESE ~~LATENT~~ BELATED EXPLANATIONS; AS TO ~~MY ACTIONS~~ THE CAUSES, AND ACTIONS, WHICH I HAVE TAKEN OVER THESE PAST WEEKS; THAT I SET FORTH TO WRITE THIS LETTER.

IV.

Would you like to do some speed with me?
Want to do some speed with me?

V.

```
God damn this motherfucking shit.
God damn this motherfucking shit.
God damn this motherfucking shit.
God damn this motherfucking shit.
God damn this motherfucking shit.
God damn this motherfucking shit.
God damn this motherfucking shit.
God damn this motherfucking shit.
God damn this motherfucking shit.
God damn this motherfucking shit.
God damn this motherfucking shit.
God damn this motherfucking shit.
God damn this motherfucking shit.
God damn this motherfucking shit.
God damn this motherfucking shit.
God damn this motherfucking shit.
God damn this motherfucking shit.
God damn this motherfucking shit.
God damn this motherfucking shit.
God damn this motherfucking shit.
God damn this motherfucking shit.
God damn this motherfucking shit.
God damn this motherfucking shit.
God damn this motherfucking shit.
```

CUCKOO

Gabe's mom lived in the Berkeley flats, near the Ashby BART station. Chain-link fences enclosed many of the one-story homes, but Gabe's mom had an open yard. She believed in neighborhood unity. Gabe pulled up to the house on his mountain bike. His laundry bag was hung over his back as though he were gunning for Santa's job.

Gabe's twin brother, Dylan, sat on the porch of the bungalow, its wide concrete columns pockmarked by rocks and BB-gun pellets. Dylan disgusted Gabe a lot of the time, but he did have balls. Last year, when their mom's boyfriend had moved out, Dylan had hung a Confederate flag in the living room window. His mom had strung Tibetan prayer flags between the porch columns to hide it, but kids flicked matches into the yard. Older kids threw eggs at the bungalow and pulled the birds-of-paradise flowers out by the roots. Soon enough the house was being stoned. Gabe took down the flag so their mom wouldn't cry. Dylan claimed it had to do with Southern pride, his Virginian heritage. Bullshit, Gabe thought.

Dylan got off the porch, walked to the sidewalk, and hoisted his body perpendicular to a lamp post. His knuckles were red and swollen from push-ups; he kept up this Army practice to be arrogant. When Dylan dropped down, Gabe punched him in the arm. It was how he showed his birth-order dominance, that ten-minute edge of being the first twin out of their mom's womb.

Dylan flicked Gabe's nose. "You have the money?" he asked.

"It's not with my dirty laundry, dipshit," Gabe said. He had some money, but didn't want to waste it on his brother. Plus, Timmy had called last night; he had relocated from Chico, in the Sacramento Valley, and wanted Gabe to get in the weed business again. He kept texting him. Gabe rolled the bike to the side of the house and locked it to the neighbor's fence. Dylan took off down the street, saying he was going to the corner store for some beers.

Gabe carried his laundry into the house. The front door opened to a wide living room with a built-in bookcase on each side of the fireplace. The cuckoo clock above the mantel spat out a bluebird. It was missing its beak. Dylan liked aiming his BB gun at it.

After Gabe put a load in the washer, he got the spackling supplies from under the sink and spread compound over the holes by the clock, swearing under his breath. Gabe preferred to leave Dylan with his own shit, but he felt bad for their mom.

For one thing, Gabe had a kid, Sam, who was nine. He felt the fatherhood guilt hard, especially with his mother's mantel was cluttered with Sam's school pictures and his clumsy ceramic turtles. He didn't bring Sam to visit Berkeley too often, since his son lived in Chico. Lately he felt nervous around Sam. It was hard to figure out what to say to him on the phone, and his kid was constantly playing games on his iPad in the background.

Besides, Gabe finally had a girl in his life, Karen. He liked sleeping with her; she moved like a Slinky, pudgy with big tits, and he didn't want his screw-ass brother to mess it up. If his mom kicked Dylan out, he'd end up living with him.

Gabe whistled quietly and went into his mom's bedroom. He opened the top drawer of the dresser, looking for loose bills.

He found Dylan at the side of the house, crouched down by Gabe's bike. He was adjusting the derailleur. The six-pack of Bud was next to him, like a puppy.

"You've got a problem," Dylan said.

"What's your point?"

"Never mind. I fixed it as best I could."

Gabe unlocked the bike, stood on it, and pushed down with his right foot. "Seems OK to me."

"The gear shifts are slow to engage. It's the derailleur. I bent it back, but don't think you owe me one. Just get me the money."

Gabe's ringer was turned off, but his phone still

buzzed. He knew it would be Timmy. He needed to think—he could think when he rode his bike. "Come over later," he said to his brother. "We'll head out for drinks."

From his mom's house, Gabe biked south on Shattuck, then southwest on MacArthur into Oakland. The boulevard, named for a general, devolved into neglected neighborhoods. College kids from Mills dipped into some blocks, sampling Hispanic or Asian food on the cheap, but for Gabe it was a ride-through—past gated convenience stores and bodegas with fruit bins and piñatas hanging from the ceilings. His mom called herself a liberal, but she never drove through MacArthur's Fruitvale district. Maybe she was scared of carjackers, drive-bys, or the hookers with thick knees who worked the burger joints' parking lots.

Gabe rode with a hitch every mile or so, the chain jerking off the derailleur. After cursing his brother, he jammed the bike on the sidewalk and turned the pedal so the chain engaged with the gear teeth. He breathed in bus and truck exhaust; the wind made his eyes tear up. Still, he felt better riding than sitting around like he used to, doing bong hits all day.

To the east, the hills rose up, embracing the flatland. The silhouette of trees formed a wave against the sky. He passed folks at bus stops, in hairnets or Raiders jackets, with anxious kids kicking at the plastic walls.

Gabe crossed against traffic, shooting up to the Redwood Hills. In the park, his bike wheels rocketed down a path. The sun was setting, but the dirt path radiated heat and kicked up dust. A lizard scrambled off a rock. Gabe rode off the trail down a smaller path, toward a stream where salmon spawned. He held on to the handles, but he had to brake to avoid hitting a tree. He spun out and fell in the dirt, his bike landing next to him. A rock tore his pants and cut his knee.

He picked up the bike and looked it over. The chain had come off again. When he attached it to the teeth, he moved the pedal to tighten it, like he had all afternoon. He wiped his greasy hands on his jeans and noticed something new. One of the nuts on the front tire fork was loose. He tightened it, thought of Dylan fixing the derailleur, and wondered, Did he loosen it? If the front tire had fallen off, Gabe could've reeled over the handlebars and onto a rock. But Dylan wouldn't have done it; he wanted the money Gabe owed him.

At Karen's, Gabe sat on the balcony overlooking the backyard. Karen was at her sister's for the weekend, so he wouldn't be hounded about the bruises and scrapes. He pretended he lived in a neighborhood that had some action. A BART train flashed by on the elevated tracks, as if rushing to someplace important, not more stops along the East Bay sprawl.

After the train passed, Gabe heard arguing from the front yard. Big Daddy was yelling and slapping his grandson again. Big Daddy, long-time occupant of the block, owned it. He was an older black guy who seemed to know all the gossip, but that wasn't shared to Gabe at first. Maybe all the gossip was a lie. Who knows? It was a crack "hotspot," according to the papers. But Gabe considered himself lucky to be out of his mom's house. He ended up here because it came with Karen. He was nothing if not an opportunist. And he didn't view that as self-criticism.

He could tune out the ruckus, and he tried to ignore the sound he knew was Dylan, pounding on the front door and yelling his name. He heard Big Daddy telling Dylan to shut up. Big Daddy liked the twins most of the time. They drank beers with him out of the cooler kept in Big Daddy's trunk. Gabe figured Big Daddy liked them in that shallow way drinkers tolerate each other across racial lines. Neither Gabe nor Dylan had been into Big Daddy's house, but Big Daddy lent Gabe his edge trimmer to keep the block looking good.

Gabe met Dylan outside, mocking the BB gun in his brother's back pocket. Big Daddy's grandson, Petey, ran over and asked for a quarter. Dylan gave him all the change in his pocket.

Gabe and Dylan headed toward a few bars they liked on University Avenue, a mile or so north. Shattuck Avenue looked static, its car dealerships quiet for the night. Shattuck, a former railroad line in the 1800s, was four lanes wide with a green median strip, and the stores' parking spaces were separated from the thoroughfare by more concrete strips: one way in, one way out. The sidewalks were vacant, except for couples out for a quiet evening. The brothers passed cheap Chinese restaurants, used bookstores, and a second-story massage parlor that never seemed to get much business.

Gabe counted the blocks that consisted of silence on his end and stories from Dylan's. His brother didn't even need a grunt or a nod to keep going. He talked about being in Iraq, about guys in his Army unit who had liked him, for the most part, but he had a couple of enemies, too. They hated him for no good reason except they wanted to be home and he rubbed them the wrong way. They're looking for you to fuck up, Dylan told him. If you stumbled, if you coughed, you heard about it for days. Dylan walked faster. He held out his BB gun.

Gabe pointed to flags waving around a car lot. "No snipers here. The only thing I want to study is the bottom of a pint."

Dylan took out his BB gun and shot it toward a street sign.

"Shit," Gabe said. He ran and laughed, then stumbled on his sore knee. Dylan helped him up.

"I don't have your money," Gabe said. "But you can have my paycheck. Serious."

At a bar on University, a couple of women noticed the twins, as they always did. They bought the pitchers. As twins, Gabe and Dylan attracted women who would do things for them, until the women learned better. Dylan lit a five-dollar bill on fire, just to see what a college chick in a halter top would do.

Gabe challenged Dylan to a game of darts. The stereo system played Rush and AC/DC. Dylan played air guitar, indifferent to people's stares. Gabe drank a soda, alternating it with the beer.

Gabe picked up a dart and steadied himself behind the line. The board was in front of a black curtain, at regulation distance. Gabe admired the Brits on TV who didn't play darts professionally until they were fat enough to rest a beer on their gut. They didn't waver, even with a cigarette hanging off their lip.

He threw the dart and it hit the outer circle. He swore, hoping no one besides Dylan saw.

Gabe flagged down a waitress for another pitcher and sat back with Dylan. He wasn't sure how to bring up the weed business. Dylan didn't approve of drugs. Then Timmy came in, looking around. Gabe waved him over. "What's that asshole doing here?" Dylan asked. Gabe told him to be quiet. No big thing.

Gabe knew Timmy from Chico. Timmy first gave him weed in elementary school and later sold pot for his own family. People erroneously believed the pot was better in Humboldt, the golden triangle, but the hotter days in Chico stressed out the plants and made the weed stronger.

Gabe was adept at business, starting with selling and trading baseball cards. He amassed good ones, like the Reds' Pete Rose and Bill "Spaceman" Lee, and sold them to buy weed in the boys' room. The math was simple. A dime equaled one gram, and an eighth was three-and-a-half, so he could buy an eighth, sell two grams at ten bucks each (back then), and have a gram and a half left to smoke.

After high school, Gabe's big break in dealing came

when Timmy figured out he could be trusted. First he was allowed to pet the dog in the front room. It was a poodle in diapers. Gabe was too high not to laugh.

During the next visit, he got to enter the living room. Timmy's dad, Stuart, was the closest Chico came to the white-trash mafia. He didn't just sell local weed; he moved it for the Mexicans. He had heavy, lidded eyes and wore a cowboy hat with a silver buckle. He sat on a couch in front of a low dining room table, facing the door. Gabe handed him a present, a book of Civil War maps. Stuart opened it to one of the Battle of Antietam. "General Lee, man," Stuart said, drawing his finger across the Confederate lines. "The genius lost his shit on that one."

Gabe took a rolling paper and dropped some of his own leaves into the crease, rolling an even joint. He brought it to his lips and Timmy shook his head, but Gabe sealed it with saliva anyway, hoping the ends wouldn't be wet. His hand shook when he handed it to Stuart, but he took a hit without coughing and handed it to one of Timmy's cousins.

For two years after high school, Gabe worked for Timmy. Every day, he slept until 1:00 p.m. His breakfast consisted of a Big Gulp and a McD burrito. When he came back and plugged in the answering machine, he jotted down five or so calls and answered the phone, which constantly rang. He made the rounds in a green Pinto, getting high with most of the people he sold to. He could buy anything he wanted, like an electronic bong that lit up purple.

Timmy poured himself a pint from the pitcher. He had bad skin and was missing a tooth. He talked quickly, confusing Dylan with Gabe.

Dylan got up to play a round of darts. Timmy stood by the board with his hand over the bullseye, daring him to throw. "Don't be a squirrel," Timmy said. "Just do it."

Dylan threw a dart. Gabe watched its arc and descent. He winced. The dart entered the board about an inch from Timmy's palm.

Timmy laughed and said, "I've been jabbed with needles thicker than this dart, buddy."

"Watch this." Dylan took out his BB gun and shot it into the center of the board. The bartender yelled over the music to get the hell out, but Timmy walked to the line and patted him on the back.

"Things will look up for you, Gabe," he said.

"I'm Dylan. I'm straight."

"It's cool," Timmy said. His words were slurred. He nodded at the college girls. "Good evening, ladies." He dropped a twenty on the table toward the tab.

The brothers staggered back to Karen's apartment after 3:00 a.m. Dylan fell asleep on the couch, and Gabe took the bed. He woke to a paper bag of empty beer bottles by the front door. Dylan was gone.

Gabe pulled back the mismatched curtains to let in some sun. Karen had gotten them from the Goodwill bin. He wasn't sure he could stay with someone who let one curtain hang down farther than the other.

In Karen's kitchen, Gabe limped to the fridge. All that walking last night after the bike accident had tweaked his knee. Gabe counted nine salad dressing bottles; most were half-empty and expired. He ran them under the sink to wash off the residue and lined them on the counter. He rubbed his eyes. He called his son, but when he heard the high-pitched voice on the outgoing message he hung up. Sometimes it was too painful.

He hadn't wanted to be a dad, but his son's mom didn't want to have another abortion. She had cried when she thought of sitting next to the vacuum machine, the little cells and bits of tissue going into the hazardous waste disposal. She couldn't go through that again. Plus, he believed they would stay together.

The phone rang—it was Dylan. He told him he took Gabe's job. He said the boss didn't care if it was one brother or another. Gabe didn't care, either. He could find another job putting in sheetrock. Construction and restaurant jobs—they were felons' occupations.

Done with housekeeping, Gabe looked through the listings for a car. He called someone named Maggie Holmes about a '73 Ford Gran Torino, green with a wide body and a 351 engine. He didn't care if it was a gas-guzzler; it was cheap, only $900. Maggie didn't know its worth. On the phone she said she had inherited it from an ex-boyfriend. Gabe listened because he felt he could talk her down even more.

He took a BART train to her house. It was a small bungalow with hydrangeas under the picture window.

She seemed a little shaken at first, like she wasn't used to having a strange man in her kitchen. She offered Gabe a beer.

"My landlady—she walks around naked sometimes."

"I'd like to see that," Gabe said.

"Yeah, but she sleeps in my bed when I'm out. She told me she has herpes. But she doesn't sleep in it when she has an outbreak."

"Damn," Gabe said, glad he didn't take a glass for his beer.

He noticed the landlady had her own bedroom, pristine, with a hippie altar and Grateful Dead bears in the corner. Gabe felt bad that Maggie, with her red-hennaed hair, had a landlady who sullied her sheets. Women shouldn't live together. It made them territorial and nutty.

But this landlady was in Belgium visiting her parents, so he could relax. On the fridge was a list of things Maggie was supposed to clean, like the tops of the doors and the light-switch plates.

"Do you want to hang out sometime? Talk about your landlady?"

"Sure," she said. "I'm off on Mondays."

But Gabe felt guilty. He wanted to stay true to Karen. He liked how this North Berkeley girl smelled, though, and how her body moved under the dress. He liked the Gran Torino, too.

He blamed his condition on being a twin—that feeling that another life similar to his was being led simultaneously, and he could never judge which one was better. There was no preferable choice, just different ones. Like when he heard his kid coughing on the phone, and he hung up, relieved he would get a good night's sleep and his kid's mother wouldn't. He felt guilt, but it passed as soon as he turned on the TV.

He said yes to the car and got Maggie to agree to a drink later that night. He liked it that her bra strap was showing, and she tried to hide it. It was compulsive, like knowing which people would buy drugs. He could tell people who were susceptible to good salesmen.

The Gran Torino ran out of gas a block away from his mom's house, under shoes dangling from the electric wires. He cursed and put the car in neutral. He forced down the window with one hand on top of the glass and the other shoving the broken handle in circles. He saw the kids down the street—the ones he was sure had torn up his mother's lawn.

He got out, as if he planned all along to get some exercise. He had to lean inside to steer, trying to push a few thousand pounds of metal and plastic down the road, not veering into the other cheap cars on either side. The kids came closer. Someone chucked an acorn at him. Then another. Then a rock. They ran behind him, aiming at his bare legs and ass.

When he lived in Chico, he used to sell weed to kids about their age. One kid with a Nike fade cut into his scalp and a ripped t-shirt sat on the hood. Gabe turned the wheel as if it to take on these kids, as if the rusted Ford vehicle with the peeling roof could become a battering ram at will. He breathed deeply and shoved the Ford, but two other boys started pushing from the trunk. Just as Gabe felt a rock hit his shoulder, he lost control of the car. It hit the side of a Toyota sedan. The impact triggered the car-alarm sensor.

Gabe knew the leader, a kid named Aja. He balanced on the rail of a fence about a few feet away. A thin boy with a Ghanaian dad and a white hippie mom, he looked graceful standing on the fence with his arms outstretched, as if he could ascend to Heaven. Instead, he bent his knees and jumped onto a stained mattress on the sidewalk.

A kid in a Bob Marley shirt pointed at Gabe and yelled above the alarm, "Your DSDD!"

"Your DSDD" meant, he was fairly certain, "your dad sucks donkey dicks." Ludicrous. He left the broken car. He ran down the sidewalk and grabbed his crotch. The gesture was too late. The boys had moved on, around the corner on their skateboards. The only people who saw his junk clutch was his mother, frizzy-haired and eating a bagel with hummus and sprouts, and his son. His son was not smiling. He had his baseball cap pulled down low.

ZÀI JIÀN

Hazel didn't invite people over. Her husband, Tom, had painted the house black before he left on tour. It was supposed to be a rebuke to bucolic Laurelhurst's set-back charm, and it did reduce the footsteps and door-bell ringing of plastic-wrapped children shaking her down for candy on Halloween. The couple balanced wise real estate decisions (buying in a good neighbor-hood in Portland) with a healthy misanthropy.

Tom put a cow's skull over the door. But Hazel took it down. She worried it would confuse pagan Burners. They might think it was an invitation for fire-licked drum circles. Some knew Tom used to drum at Anton LaVey's house parties back in San Francisco. She never went. They were racists. No amount of punk fashion could hide the fact she was Chinese. Tom had said: "They're being ironic. Besides, Anton's LPs are collector's items."

She put a large NO SOLICITORS sign over the

door. Plus their dog sounded like Satan's pet when he barked.

Then Hazel's mother moved in. She didn't have anywhere else to go. She held her suitcase in front of her as a shield against the dog.

One night, fingers rubbed across the skin of Hazel's face. Ears picked up vibrations. Do ears have knowledge of a personal sound versus a stranger's sound? Her skin was rough. She felt across wrinkles. To the hairline where lice once shit and bred.

"Hazel!" Her mom said her name like each syllable was a ring tone on the phone. It was 3:00 a.m. The dog barked and put his paws on the window above Hazel's bed.

Hazel wrapped the bathrobe around her. She shut the door on the dog. He scratched and whined to be let out. She walked down the hall, scaring herself. But what was there to be scared of? It was only her mother.

Her mother increased the repetition of her name. Hazel hated the sound of it coming from her mother. Raspy. Her mother added her middle name, Mei (the orphanage name). Then her last name.

Hazel opened the guestroom door slowly and turned on the light. She had always studied her mom. She was the daughter-in-waiting. The woman-in-waiting. Blood dripping. Eyes glowing from the closet. The cat's eyes, peeing on the laundry. She was small and her mom was ever growing.

Hazel bent down to hear her mother's breath. Her

mother put a hand on Hazel's neck. She lifted Hazel's chin and stared at her. She plucked a hair with tweezers.

"Ow!" Hazel said.

"Damn it," her mother said. "That was bothering me all day."

"Mom, you need to sleep."

"Give me a huggy-bug."

Hazel rubbed her eyes. Trains were bringing in Chinese goods from container ships all night long. She'd heard train whistles all her life, even used to travel on boxcars from El Cerrito up to Portland when her head was shaved. She remembered them from when she walked along the railroad lines picking up iron ties. She carried them in her Army coat, thinking she could hit someone in the head if he tried to rape her.

In the old days, Chinese rail workers wrapped up the bones of the dead and sent them back to China. They went by train, then by ship.

In 1868, a schooner sailed from San Francisco with thirty-nine boxes of Chinese remains and traveled back to the home villages. So the ghosts would rest.

She had no place to send her bones. No known village. No known mother besides this one here. The remains of the females rotted in the sun. They weren't important. Only the men were shipped back.

She tucked her mother in and kissed her on the forehead. "Goodbye," she whispered in Mandarin. There were ten different ways of saying this simple word. For all her mother knew, she was saying, "Goodnight."

PRELUDE TO A KISS

Walk into the party. Try not to look at the couch with the Afghan blanket over the top, another piece of furniture the cat ripped up. You will not sit there. You will never get up again. You'll fall into the cushions and dogs will eat your corpse. Your butt will grow instantly from the size it was at age seventeen to the size it will be twenty years later, but the rest of your body will stay the same. Your butt will be glutinous and firm in places where the squats have had an effect, but wide. You could turn each cheek into a bird feeder. Sprinkle suet on top.

You sit anyway, super-glued to the polycotton fabric. You do a bong hit of a crushed Quaalude. It feels like plastic is coating your lungs. Not a good idea.

You pass around a handmade pipe, trying to ingratiate yourself with the friends of your new boyfriend: roofers and bikers and petty ex-cons. It's the pipe that Fred—boyfriend #1—made you in shop class. He found a scrap piece of cedar and carved and sanded it for you, bought you a screen for the top. The pipe goes around the circle and never makes it back to you. You are too high to notice. Guns are under beds. Dogs sleep in corners.

You don't believe in karma, except when something bad happens. You're cheating on Fred with Billy—boyfriend #2—no wonder the pipe disappears.

You break up with Fred, and he says on the phone, heartbroken, "Ralph said I could shoot you with his rifle."

Now, much older, you walk down the street with no sidewalks in Virginia, past the burned-down antique mall, the cement factory, and the auto repair store. You walk on a yellow-slabbed path to the bike trail, the old C&O canal. You stop in front of the Masonic Temple, a brick faux-Colonial building, with no erect bushes or spherical shrubbery by the entrance. Just white trim and harsh bricks and the Masonic emblem centered above the first story. The compass spreads out, intertwined with a square, and a side rule underneath. The *G* in the middle. The goal. The G-spot.

Questions of Masonic wives: Will he have to ride a goat? Is it evil? Why does he have to wear an apron?

The Masons don't recruit you, though you lost your virginity in their shadow, and you don't marry Fred. His spit tastes bad—pot mixed with the tang of Crest toothpaste. He sucks your tongue hard in the parked car, and it doesn't feel good.

The Pinto is on your side. The Pinto with its puke-green exterior and the inside that smells of spilled soda and milk, not with the patina of child, but of teen-boy. Crusted catsup packs from late-night stoner runs to a hamburger place; cassette tape of Lou Reed's *Rock n Roll Animal*—with the song "Heroin." On the cover, Lou looks nothing like your boyhood crush, David Cassidy. The orange-lit skin, the blurry metal necklace, the studded bracelet, the mic cord wrapped around another wrist. Lou looks to the side with black lips. He will not pose with a horse. He will not ask you to join his fan club.

You take the lyrics of "Heroin" literally, like a bedtime story, with the simple, arpeggiated guitar chords. "Jesus' Son. Hair. Oh. In. It's my wife and it's my life. Leads to a center in my head. And then I'm better off dead."

You are scared of needles. You back away. Even though Billy sometimes stays with Willis, whose walls and aquarium are covered with blood tracks. You think it looks like an art installation made of fake blood—the set of a splatter film. But it's real blood shot out from a syringe. Gay porn cartoons are drawn on the bathroom wall during junkie constipation. The kitchen has a blackened spoon. Willis eats pizza every day and works at a hotel at night. You borrow Burroughs from him. You read *Basketball Diaries*. He mocks you.

He thinks you should work at his hotel as a whore for Arab tourists. He is in love with Billy. Of course he mocks you. You bring him an anti-drug poster from the Falls Church Police Department. Willis studies it to see if there's anything he's missed, if there's any description that seems incorrect. You wear white pants and a buttoned shirt. He signs your yearbook in blood, writing, *Art is anything you can get away with—Andy Warhol.*

At home you practice Chopin, the repetitive notes under modulating chords. A procession to a cemetery, graves covered with moss.

Your teacher says, "You can't play his Preludes unless you experience pain." You will find that pain.

ANGEL DUST

I.

Gib holds his pee and doesn't laugh when one kid stutters on the rug. He chews and tries to swallow mustard-flavored meat. Aiden calls him short. That is first grade.

Third grade. Gib comes home and cries about the bullying. Shrimp Little Dinky. He wants to kick things, but his sister Liza strokes his hair, says no. He spits on the bed through the sheets, drooling hate in the flavors of watermelon and peanut butter.

II.

I pound on the cab's steering wheel. Sarah digs a pencil into her leg. She wants to know me because she's tasted me.

III.

My sister Liza, now dead, never teased me for playing with a stick. Oak. Maple. Hickory. The stick had a name, transferred to others as they broke in snake or gopher holes, or were tossed off the overpass. Liza, the orange lollipop, knew the stick's name.

How can I tell my girlfriend the secret name, her breath frosting the window, when she fears me?

IV.

Their father, a career NSA spy, slaps hellos. Belts goodbyes. Seven is too many. They start dying. Anorexia takes the first one, Liza. Six left.

This burger is the best comfort food. Radio off!

Gib's girlfriend pays for cab repairs. Gib has a long tongue. He says he once gave a ride to Idi Amin. He sold drugs to hookers. He got robbed in Anacostia. He tells his girlfriend he knew the color of his boss's sheets. Lies tumble from his mouth, now with all his teeth, then with fewer.

V.

"I had to wipe my nose twenty times in each class. I sniffled a hundred more. I coughed a lot."

"Does that mean you want to sleep with me?"

"My throat hurts."

"Turn off the flashlight."

"Look at the shadows."

"It's irritating my eyes."

"Are there fairies in-between the slats of the blinds?"

"Sure. One of them is Liza, watching you."

VI.

I unplug the TV but the sound keeps going: *Leave the jokes to me, Chuckles.*

I have pot sex with Sarah. The one who smells like my dead candy sister. And I have Dilaudid sex with him. We spatter blood on the aquarium and on the walls. Cockroaches descend into Pepsi bottles. Is this love?

Oh, another wrinkle cream with no urgency in making any change happen whatsoever.

I tie up my German shepherd outside the gay bathhouse on St. Mark's Place.

It's better to give than to receive.

VII.

Bodies falling. Drowning. Shot dead in the water. Soldiers stepping on uniformed corpses in the churning tide.

"Are you upset about the violence?" my remaining sister asks her son.

"It's a movie."

"Maybe not so good here."

My nephew shuts off his iPad.

I am the host. My skin yellowed by hep C. No one was supposed to know. My nephew sips a Frappuccino, tonguing sugary goo.

No one hands me a stick to caress as a guide toward death. Neither oak, nor maple, nor hickory.

VIII.

The sand cools when the storm comes. Translucent insects flatten to survive. I hold bones of desiccated crabs pressed into tire tracks that course over me. I can't express pain, but it is visible during lightning flares. Thunder follows, deafening. It opens a space between the water below—of salt, fish, and bone fragments from an anorexic—and the air tumid with water and wind. Ions shudder.

EXIT

If you see a tall building in Portland, do you feel embarrassed for it? The striving, the corporate fuckitude looking down with glinted windows on a river polluted with shit and industrial waste, glided over by dragon boaters?

When you cross a bridge, do you remember walking across with your son, guiding him over the scary view of river beneath the concrete? Clanging metal wires and grids. Waves. Car exhaust?

Your neural tangles binding and strengthening with thoughts of true skyscrapers left behind in the old life (San Francisco) and acceptance of a less dramatic life (Portland) with your younger son (forever blending in time and space) and your husband (who pierced you first at age twenty-five with a needle and ink). You and your husband clasp veiny hands and baby hands together and say in unison on the sidewalk: "One, two, three, up!" You both lift him, and he is secure with you (he does not want to break the mother's back). A childhood of jumping. Again! It is his joy.

Do you hear the word *jump* and wince?

Do you remember the arrow thrust of that word from your husband's lips? How that arrow pierced you and you cried out in public?

How he blames you later for driving him to the hospital. (I did not need to go to the ER. You made me go.)

How he blames you later for outpatient care. (You made me go to crazy camp.)

How you had to call your wedding minister from the Church of the Sub-Genius, breaking your husband's privacy. You should be on the outside with your people. Your minister is his best friend. The singer of his former punk band turned corporate. You call, smoothing grime and cat hair from your shoes into sidewalks around your home, saying: "He's sleeping all day. He says he wishes he'd killed himself three months ago. He's living only for his son. What should I do when he wakes? What should I do? What should I do?" (Remember: If he blames you later, he said he had the desire. He said he had the plan.)

The public space: emergency room. He is handing over the insurance card. He has no job. Handing over your fate to more debt. Handing over your private heart to a social worker, intermediating between the two of you. The skin on skin severed. The heartbeat on heartbeat severed. The pen, instead, carving words onto the paper.

What: The social worker says to you on the vinyl cushion that the contrast between living with you (domineering, poisonous) and being in love (unsaid: with a true artist) is too much. (You don't need to refer to the exact words. You know, even as you'd seduced him two days before, even as he'd cried on your chest, wetting your t-shirt, because his love crush had a boyfriend.) A woman overhears. Says her husband's even worse.

Admitting nurse. What: Do you have thoughts of self-harm?

He says: Yes.

Admitting nurse. What: Do you have a plan?

He says: Jump.

He won't tell you where. It is his secret.

SEX BOMB

Do they have to cut open my penis parts to get the sperm out?

So you pee it out in a cup and pour it on the egg?

So it gets out of the cup and searches around and finds the egg and tells the other sperms and they all jump into it?

So what do they do? They wait until they're eighteen and kiss and hug and then start pooping out eggs and sperm?

Do they hide in a room and lock the door because they don't want to be embarrassed that they're pooping out eggs and sperm?

How do the eggs get back in? Do they jump into the last cup of pee and jump onto a vagina hair and open a trapdoor and get in?

To make a baby, you cut a hole in Dad's nuts and put a tube in, then cut a hole in Mom's stomach and get the egg out. You put a crack in it, then the egg sucks up the sperm. Then you take the tube out from Dad and patch it up, then patch Mom up. Then Mom sits on the egg.

The egg peeks out of the woman's mouth, like Jerry by his mouse hole. And Tom the sperm and his fellow soldiers swarm out of the man's butt. They hold on to the woman's pubic hair and pull themselves inside her. That one sperm, Tom, finds the egg and smashes it. And that is how the baby is made.

FALLEN NEST

Cookie checked her phone messages from a pay phone, one of the last ones in Portland, she guessed. She had parked by a Laundromat, much to her daughter Molly's dismay. Molly hated errands with that narcissism of youth. Cookie didn't have pity, though, because Molly had dropped her cell phone in the toilet that morning. Molly held onto Cookie's pants and cried, then slapped at her when she tried to pick her up. Cookie looked away, gathering her breath. She didn't want to panic with this four-year-old creature, this person who took up most of her brain and made it stupid. She zipped up Molly's green parka and ripped out a page from the phone book for something Molly could destroy.

Cookie forwarded through her messages, but no one had left a new one. She let Molly hit her. Maybe, magically, the pain would reach Gretchen, her first daughter, and she would call again, defending her poor mom. They had talked the night before, after Molly had fallen asleep. Gretchen had gotten Cookie's number from Paul, her birth father. She knew the correct adoption lingo. She had a dad, an anthropology professor at Berkeley; she had a birth father, who moved desks around in a used office furniture store. Now she wanted Cookie, her birth mother. Cookie never thought of Paul as a "birth father," just as the guy who had once declared his love for her on a paper bag. She kept the bag in a metal box, but she hadn't spoken to him in years.

She didn't have the nerve to call Gretchen back, not knowing if the number she had left was her parents' or hers. She wondered what habits Gretchen had. Her lost baby, now thirteen.

But Molly took her attention, not letting her complete the simple, obsessive task of redialing. Cookie pulled her back from the curb. "I'm going to count to five," she said. "Then you're going to have to do what I say."

"Onetwothreefourfive," Molly said. "I said it. What are you going to do?" Her black pigtails stuck out like bat wings. She slapped Cookie again.

At the bus stop by the pay phone, a woman in a gray coat and yoga pants glared at them. She should've been looking for the bus, as if looking would make it arrive ahead of schedule, but she twisted her mouth and said to Cookie, "The best way to enrage a child is to avoid looking in her eyes."

Cookie frowned, confused. She didn't have to look

at Molly to know she was there. Every breath was folded up in Molly's screams. The woman smiled, as if expecting Cookie to thank her.

The woman opened her purse and fumbled inside it, pulling out a crinkled Hershey's Kiss. "Is it OK if I give her some chocolate?"

Molly accepted it, shyly, and shoved it in her mouth.

"Thanks," Cookie said, hating herself for letting a stranger intimidate her. She put Molly, complaining, into the car seat, but forgave her when she fell asleep, her tiny fist curled around printed names from the white pages.

Cookie drove to her father's house, a cabin outside Portland. He agreed to look after Molly so Cookie could go to a First Mothers' meeting, for women who had given up their children for adoption. She wasn't even supposed to use the phrase "given up." She was supposed to feel positive about her choice. In the adoption world, all her choices were supposed to have arisen from love, not fear or self-loathing. She wondered about mothers, their many failings, though her father, Bud, wasn't much better.

Bud didn't trust people who were punctual, so Cookie took Molly to a creek, bubbling with motor oil and antifreeze. Molly ran to the bridge and climbed up on the railing, her tights snagging on the wood. She balanced with her arms dangling over, and Cookie didn't stop her. She was too old to think she could win with fate. She called, "Be careful," as an afterthought.

Molly swayed, shouting, "I'm a fairy!" She fluttered her hands and Cookie ran to her. She pulled Molly down and shook her arm.

"Don't you listen to anything I say anymore?" Cookie said. Such a force of will poured out from Molly. She was fearless where Cookie was not anymore. When Cookie became a mom, she lost her singularity: her skin, breasts, eyes, ears, and mouth—even the first time, with Gretchen, the baby she didn't keep or name. Molly wrapped her arms around Cookie's neck and kissed her with sour-juice breath. Cookie murmured secret names into her daughter's hair.

If you're cold, you take your mittens off for your child. You give her your last piece of cake. You try to be less selfish, but only for her. You feign interest in other friends' children. It doesn't work.

Inside Bud's house, Cookie and Molly negotiated around boxes of cassette tapes, stacks of newspapers, and socialist journals. The front room smelled of cigarettes and peanut butter. Coffee mugs were made into makeshift ashtrays, balanced on bookshelves and sofa arms.

Cookie had called her dad "Bud" since she was little, because he said "Dad" was patriarchal. But he couldn't erase her deference to him by insisting on a name change or inviting her to smoke pot with him and his friends.

Cookie told Molly to run to the backyard. She liked to play among the shopping carts arranged with shells and animal bones.

Bud got Cookie a soda and ruffled her hair. "Don't bother with duct tape," he said to her, as if they had been talking politics the whole time. He listened to the public stations at the bottom of the dial. He told her, as if she didn't know, that the Homeland Security Threat Level was currently Orange. The government was warning the public to stock duct tape and cans of food in case of a terrorist bioattack.

"It's ridiculous," he said. "All we have to do is have enough duct tape to seal off the basements? Then what? We'll die of oxygen deprivation."

"I have a bumper sticker for you—it's a free idea," Cookie said. "You'll love it. 'You can't duct-tape freedom.' Sell it on the Internet." She wondered how to bring up money. It was bad enough he knew about the First Mothers' group. He called it a "cult of pain."

Then Molly screamed. Cookie ran toward the sound and found her daughter in the back room, hidden under a red blanket.

Cookie ripped it off. Molly's striped dress was pulled over her knees. Bo-peep and the little sheep circled the base of a bedroom lamp. Molly had her fingers in her mouth. The light bulb was missing, exposing the socket. Molly had shocked herself. "It felt like hot pokes," she said.

Cookie looked at the apple juice spilled on the rug, covering older stains.

How could she bring another daughter to this life? Maybe between loans from Bud and her mother she could get enough money to fix up her apartment and make it suitable for Gretchen, whose toes were so long and elegant, even at two days old.

She took Molly to the kitchen, checking for anything she might eat for dinner. She found ice cream, which would appease her daughter during the farewell.

Bud sat at his desk, transcribing a tape. His hair was thinning and gray, and his socks looked dirty sticking out from his sandals. "Can I bring you some food?" Cookie asked. "You don't have any vegetables."

That night, at the First Mothers' meeting, Cookie gripped a coffee cup in the ceramics room that smelled of damp clay and glaze. Next door, she could hear square dancers doing the do-si-do. She let the coffee cool while women introduced themselves, some knitting, others staring with pinched eyes. They urged her to post to their website and donate to candidates who supported adoption rights. The circle they made with their metal chairs reminded her of being in Sunday school, trying to feel God's presence from Bible songs and prune juice, only they were channeling their missing children.

Someone asked what she did for a living. "I'm a medical transcriber," she said. Her job description stopped most conversations. Cookie was surprised that a lot of the women went on to have more children. She told them about the social worker who had helped her after the adoption, and why she had moved north from Berkeley to Portland—to get away from the hospital and everything associated with it.

The woman in charge of the meeting handed out a list of books and movies that people in the adoption world should avoid, like the children's book *Are You My Mother?* Cookie rolled her eyes, as if a child would read about a lost, confused baby bird and be traumatized, as if that were all it took.

When Cookie was twelve, a robin had built a nest in a crook of a butterfly bush, its branches low and thick. The nest was made of packed dirt and branches, with strands of green plastic webbing hanging down. A cat climbed the branch and the robin flew to the fence. Did the bird watch? Cookie didn't know.

The cat knocked the pale-blue egg out of the nest. It cracked open on the grass. The fetus was orange-yellow curled like a crooked finger. Cookie yelled at the cat and chased it away. She picked up the egg, and ooze covering the fetus spread across her palm. She dug a hole in loose dirt near the tree. The cat crept back and sat closely, its tail twitching. Cookie didn't understand. The cat got fed every day from a can, so why did it have to kill?

The robin abandoned the nest because it was compromised. Cookie planned revenge. Before she could act, however, the cat ran away. She knocked on neighbors' doors and put up flyers for her mom's sake. For weeks, she went to the porch and scooped out cat food, imagining the bodies of beakless chickens in cat-food factories, getting chopped by mechanical knives.

Cookie finally saved money to take the Greyhound with Molly from Oregon to Berkeley. Her mother, Anne, still lived there. She seemed concerned for Cookie, that meeting Gretchen would be a bad idea. Gretchen's parents insisted that Gretchen meet Cookie and Molly alone first, and they would join them later.

Cookie had chosen a restaurant she used to go to with Paul, back when he would follow her anywhere, back when he made her cassette tapes whose covers were inscribed with blood pricked from his thumb. He was too much of a good thing, she had realized. She had left him for Molly's dad, another mistake.

The café in Berkeley had not changed in twenty years. It had large corner windows, and its deep benches invited long meals. Cookie recognized Gretchen, and she felt out of breath. At thirteen, Gretchen had wavy hair and light-brown skin, more like Paul than anyone in Cookie's family. She seemed self-assured, wearing lacy, fingerless gloves and large hoop earrings. Cookie hugged her but sat across from Gretchen, unsure of the rules. There were no rules for meeting a teenager who had come out of your womb, who had kicked against your uterine muscles, whose nutrients she had sucked from you, like a parasite.

Molly determined her own rules. She refused to sit by Cookie. She climbed under the table and sat next to Gretchen. Gretchen poured out all the crayons for her to sort.

Cookie ordered cheese blintzes with applesauce for herself and a fried egg for Molly, resisting the impulse to criticize when Molly cut out the yolk and put it on the table. The refills were free, and the more coffee

Cookie drank, the more reckless her questions became.

"Is there any secret you'd like to tell me?" she asked.

"I hate my name," Gretchen said.

"Me, too," Molly said. Cookie knew that anything this wondrous creature would hate, Molly would hate, too.

"It's a good name," Cookie said.

"I think it's old-fashioned. I want to change it, but I don't want to hurt my mom's, I mean, Katie's, feelings," Gretchen said. Cookie patted her on the hand, reassuring her.

Molly finished crayoning the kids menu and gave it to Gretchen, calling her "sister." Cookie let Molly empty packets of Sweet'n Low into her milk to keep her from interrupting or upstaging her.

"What was your childhood like?" Gretchen asked. She sounded polite, as if a therapist had asked her to show an interest.

"I have a secret I never told my own mom," Cookie said, pausing to gauge Gretchen's response. "On a dare, I stole a box of brownie mix. When I made it with my friend after school, it was delicious." Sharing this transgression was like teaching Molly to say "Satan" when she was two, for Halloween. She got bored being a good mom. Gretchen laughed.

"I thought it might taste bad because it wasn't paid for," Cookie said. "Maybe it smelled better, I don't know. But you shouldn't shoplift. It's not easy these days. You should be a good girl." She poured more sugar in her coffee. "Don't tell my mom that story when you meet her, either. And God knows don't tell your parents. You can tell my dad, Bud, if you meet him. He's an anarchist."

Gretchen got milk on her upper lip, but Cookie didn't tell her to wipe it off. She lacked the nerve. Gretchen's phone rang once, and Cookie guessed she felt shy talking to her parents in front of her. She cupped her hand when she said, "I love you," but Cookie heard.

Cookie asked what Gretchen liked to do. Horses. She liked to ride horses in Lafayette, east of Berkeley, she told her. She liked Taekwondo too. Cookie wanted to look at her feet, to see if they were still long and skinny. She tried to focus on the moment and not collect details for the next First Mothers' meeting. Apparently, Paul had gotten back in touch with their daughter more than a year ago. He hadn't forgiven Cookie enough to tell her.

"What should I call you?" Gretchen asked. "My parents said to call you what you want to be called. I don't care. I have a friend whose mothers are gay. She calls them 'Mom Denise' and 'Mom Lenore.' It's cool. Or kids with stepparents. Whatever."

Cookie blushed. "I don't know. 'Frances,' maybe? That's my real name."

"Call her 'Mom,'" Molly said. "You're my sister."

That afternoon they went to Gretchen's Taekwondo match with Gretchen's parents. The demonstrations and sparring sessions were held in a high school gym, in areas marked off by tape and plastic chairs for the judges. Cookie didn't want to like the couple, but Katie, Gretchen's mom, gave Molly snacks and seemed sweetly spacey, as if she would rather be home making apple crisp. She wore wire-rimmed glasses and pearl earrings. The dad, Jim, wore similar glasses, with that habit of middle-aged, married couples, looking like siblings. He did a crossword puzzle and didn't ask personal questions. They didn't bring cameras like the other parents. For all anyone knew, Cookie could be a visiting cousin; she was only seventeen years older than Gretchen.

Gretchen took off her shoes for the match. Her feet were slender and her legs looked strong. Cookie didn't want to feel like a breeder, evaluating her genes. She noticed Gretchen had written a "C" on the inside of her wrist. "The 'C' will bring me luck," Gretchen said. "For 'Cookie.'"

Cookie figured she would never return to this gym, so she showed Gretchen the tattoo on her stomach, of an octopus she had gotten after Molly was born. Cookie told her random things, seeing what might sink in.

Gretchen had her hair up in a ponytail, a mass of curls. Her belt was tight around her tall, slender body. When the match started she yelled and punched her opponent, a stocky girl with purple hair, who blocked her and punched her in the chest. Cookie stood up, wanting to defend her. Gretchen doubled over, losing more points.

In the next round, Gretchen and the other girl faced each other, balanced on the balls of their feet. Gretchen did a high roundhouse kick. It connected to the other girl's mouth. The girl cried when the judges gave the match to Gretchen.

She hobbled back to the bleachers. She had a half-moon-shaped indent of the other girl's teeth on her foot. Katie put ice on it and comforted her. Gretchen suddenly lost her adolescent confidence and seemed like a young girl, in her pain and desire for her mother. Their connection was primal; even Jim seemed excluded. Cookie held Molly between her legs, keeping her out of the way, but Molly relaxed into the maternal prison—her magic prison.

That night at her mom's house, Cookie lay down with Molly on a futon, which smelled of dust and cats. Molly asked whether they could live with Gretchen, but Cookie said no. They talked about Molly's birth, from an egg, like baby birds and kittens.

"How many eggs are in you now?" Molly asked.

"Two."

"Why? I don't want you to have any babies."

"I won't have any babies," Cookie said. She had gotten her tubes tied after Molly was born, but Molly, of course, didn't know that.

"Where are the eggs?

"In my uterus."

"Where is your 'universe'?" Molly said.

"Under my belly button," Cookie said.

Molly frowned. "I don't want you to have any

more babies. I already came out of your egg. I want Gretchen." After Cookie turned on a Mickey Mouse nightlight, Molly pulled up Cookie's flannel shirt to touch her navel and the octopus tattoo, which stretched over her womb. The black tentacles protected the eggs that grew and dissolved into nothing.

AFTERWORD

In 1976, the spring of fifth grade, near my hometown of Falls Church, VA, a stranger had tied Kenny to a tree. His corpse was found a few days later.

Foot down on bike pedal, then I breathe hard uphill. My hands are lined with black grease. I finally have a ten-speed! Shift gear. Bike freezes. The chain has fallen off again. Goddamn it. Fix chain. Head off. The wind rushes in my ears. I'm twelve. In seventh grade. Most of my body is vague mush except for blood and menstrual cramps.

Construction workers whistling at girls like me on bikes. Drivers honking and whistling at girls like me on bikes. Pants riding up our butts.

Dry eyes. Split lip. Stitches. Scabs. Boils. Snot. Snarled hair. Body odor. Scratches. Coughing. Phlegm.

Autumn. 1977. Seventh grade. Queen Bee, follow me. In this case, Carey Mallon, the instigator, was Queen. She had brown eyes and wore her blonde hair in a bad-girl shag.

At twelve, glasses and all, I inserted myself into a two-girl friendship, with their tacit permission; I wasn't a threat. I'd left my stuccoed home where people were sorting nails, screws, rivets, and washers into the plastic drawers of a toolbox, or cleaning the gunk out of the vegetable drawer. Our dog lay in the grass with stray gnats for company.

I climbed up to a low branch by the churchyard. The limbs had deep grooves in them. They had no opinions. I wasn't too removed from the days when I believed the sun could see me. I still believed God could see me; I liked to twist the cord around my large cross from choir.

Carey got bored on the tree so we found a younger boy to torment. We stole Randolph Dunn's skateboard and skated down Buxton Street. Girls were good at stealing. We slipped blue eyeshadow packets up the sleeves of our polyester jackets; we grabbed 7-Eleven matches to smoke our mother's cigarettes. We wanted speed and we found it; we liked to sled on snow days with older boys who tried to ram the weaker kids into parked cars. On fall days like this, we skateboarded or rode bikes. We were in an adolescent tribe and wouldn't leave until we started to date and molder in smaller packets. Then we'd be forced to listen to *Dark Side of the Moon* for the millionth time with guys who carved pot pipes in shop class. Older teenage boys would soon pull us into their orbit and flatten us. But not yet.

Speeding down tree-lined, gray streets made us hungry, so we made macaroni. It was good. I liked food. All day we ate—creamy macaroni, cake, icing, caramel apples, soda, crackers, squirtable cheese, fried baloney, Pop Tarts. If I could spoon something out of a jar, life was good.

The Smolinski boys and Eric rode on their bikes up to Carey. Eric pinched Carey's butt! She said, "My butt is swelling." I feared the boys with pimples would end up being my partner during the Virginia Reel, or animal ones would throw rocks at me again. I knew about sex from reading *Rich Man, Poor Man* from the library and *Penthouse* "Forum" letters stolen from friends' dads and older brothers. Sometimes women rode bikes without wearing underwear. They rode toward dates with a diaphragm stuck up them (though how that piece of throat was supposed to be useful in a vagina still confused me). My cousin punched me in the stomach after I asked him what wet dreams were like. I knew my body. The boils. The smells. The lines on my legs from dragging a rock across my thighs when I was lonely. Wet bathing suits wrinkled my nipples. And now Carey's butt was swelling—Eric liked it.

The same neighborhood, but dark. Halloween. There were shadows and men in cars who might kidnap me and harm me with long, hairy fingers. I wore my Joan of Arc costume—a robe, tunic, and a cardboard sword and shield. Despite my fears, I joined the horde whose fierceness was brief, hormonal, terminal. New hordes would always take over, and they'd obliterate the ones that came before.

Tom Clinton had a bottle of orange juice and vodka. Kerry Kerrico and Rob Arnold attacked us with shaving cream bottles. Tommy Green broke the glass on a lamp post with his baseball bat, and we threw eggs at parked cars. I took off my Joan of Arc robe because I thought it would get slit by a knife.

I headed home alone for eight long blocks, my bag full, my eyes straining at the bushes, the shadows behind the trees, and the ache of a headlight coming around the corner. How much time did I have till it reached me? Time enough to run to a house. What if the people in that house were bad, too? I didn't trust anyone.

At the end of fifth grade, in 1976, Kenny had met a man and a boy at a food mart. That's what I thought. His mother, a single mom, worked at the mall, at the makeup counter of J.C. Penney. Maybe Kenny sat a round plastic table by some trashcans, flipping through a comic book. His bangs fell in his face. The man, a stranger, asked him if he liked bikes. The man bought the boys ice cream. The man's son was quiet, but seemed nice. They went out to the woods behind the mall. They were going to ride racing bikes. Any boy would do that.

We sat on the Spoffords' back porch, and I let the relish and ketchup and mustard from my hot dog drip on my fingers for a long time before I licked them off.

Mrs. Spofford told us what had happened. I'd lived in Cambridge, MA, the year Kenny was killed, with my parents and younger sister and brother: another blond boy like Kenny. But now we were back in my hometown.

Girls whispered what happened, too. I heard he was tied up to a tree, raped, and strangled, and the little boy was right there. His name was Billy. He saw everything. Kenny was left in the woods (his death site now paved over for the commercial glitter plunder of Tyson's II shopping mall).

The murderer's name was Arthur Goode. When Arthur took Billy and tried to get yard work from a lady in Falls Church, the woman recognized Billy as the missing boy from the TV news, called the police, and Arthur was arrested.

But maybe Kenny wasn't picked up at the mall. Maybe he was on a newspaper route and Arthur talked him into taking a bus out to the mall. Serial killer blogs are full of errors. One says Kenny was nine. But we were both eleven. We'd been in kindergarten together, back when I was so shy I barely spoke.

"He was in my class," Denise said, years later. "He was at Seven Corners, on his bike. The guy who lured him into his van, I think with a puppy? I remember the news when he was found. I was very scared."

Tom—the kid who'd brought vodka out on that Halloween night—said Kenny was walking to school and either got into Arthur's car or was abducted. And Kenny was found naked with a belt around his neck and a severed penis in his mouth.

Was that mutilation true?

At the end of fifth grade, Tom and the other kids had passed around a poster-sized card to sign for the family.

Tom said, years later: "He was pretty quiet but was a good kickball player. He always wore a jeans jacket. It could have been any of us."

Denise remembered, "He was a cute, floppy haired kid. I liked him. Not 'liking,' liking."

Goode was executed on April 15, 1984, for the murder of the first boy he'd killed: a boy from Florida. For his taunting of the parents of the two boys he killed, Goode was the most hated man on Death Row. Even Ted Bundy stole his cookies.

In my hometown, no one talked about Kenny in sixth grade, seventh grade, or any other grade. We talked about him only as adults. The boogieman knew what boys wanted—what we all wanted—speed. Bikes. Woods. And he left us all with fear. We rode our bikes on the fastest routes through town: especially an abandoned railroad line paved over into a bike trail. Before good health infected America, the trail was often empty. We couldn't see who was around the corner or in the weeds by the polluted creek. Or running out from under the bridge. Or climbing out of a cement drainage pipe.

I didn't cure my extreme fear until I went on a two-week bike ride after eighth grade with another tribe, mostly boys. We stayed in youth hostels and rolled out our bed sheets to avoid lice and grime. My kerchief that I wore around my head to hide my frizzy hair got rolled into a headband, a style one kid called a "do drugs." I was up in Connecticut and Cape Cod with almost no supervision. I rode for hours, hitchhiked in Nantucket, smoked weak pot, and got my ears double-pierced. But I was still scared. In college, I thought punk rock would cure me.

Yet in my fifties, I still had that fear. In 2015, at a writing residency at Sou'wester Lodge, in Seaside, WA, I borrowed a bike one day and took a winding path through fields of dry grass above the beach. It would be "real" to get exercise in my slothful, grieving state—my marriage was fracturing.

I rode on the "Lewis and Clark Discovery Trail" and used habits to gauge how quickly I could dump the bike, run through the grass and sand, and reach the waves if a man attacked me. Should I drown or be strangled? I called it the "'Discover Rape' Trail." But I saw only doughy people with junk food for the seagulls. I kept riding.

FEEDBACK

"I havent read it, but Alex has really good tits for her age!" –**Cormac McCarthy**

"The characters are sociopaths and I don't like them. I have no emotional reason to care about these people."
–**Member of writing workshop, 2013**

"If you knew you had only nine months to live, you would be required to write something important.
–**Member of writing workshop, 2013**

"You say you're married?" –**Member of writing workshop, 2004**

"Your obvious skill as a writer is undeniable, and we can certainly appreciate your commitment to place-based writing and your robust depiction of city life in the Pacific Northwest. Your stories are crafted with unforgettable imagery and filled with compelling story lines unique to your voice. While a handful of the stories included in your collection handle its heavy subject matter with dignity and poignancy, some of them rely on the reader to find humor in the characters' depravity and misfortune—a result less filled with color but with a provocative, unnatural feeling." –**Acquisitions, Ooligan Press, 2010**

"My therapist is trying to get me to see that other people may not have the judgments about me that I do and that I should make peace with things that torment me. When I make judgments about myself or perceive that others are judging me, it's not the ultimate truth. Anyway, I'm sorry the church woman was critical of you, but you shouldn't hold onto it, if possible. She sounds like a bitch." –**Email to sister, 2001**

Credits

"The Courtship of Eddie's Father" was published in *Portland Review*, vol. 52, no. 3, 2005. "The Courtship of Eddie's Father" and "Fallen Nest" were performed at the Federal Bar in Los Angeles on July, 10, 2016, as part of the New Short Fiction Series, Northern Writes: Round 1, and were sold as single stories through Barnes & Noble Nook Press.

"The Desperate Ones" appeared in *Street Debris*, 2000.

"My Martian Launderette" was published in *Propeller*, summer 2010.

"The Passenger" was published in *VoiceCatcher*, summer 2016.

"Prelude to a Kiss" was published in *Watershed Review*, winter 2015.

"The Scorpion" was published in *Irreverent Fish*, spring 2008.

"The Shrew of D.C." was published in *Word Riot*, 2007.

"Teenage Riot": parts appeared in the fanzine *Bananafish* and in my script for the comedy show *Mortified.* See also "Looking Back Mortified: Why Should We Betray Our Younger Self?" *Propeller*, January 20, 2010.

"Wet" was published in *Nailed*, August 2017.

"Angel Dust" was published in *The Gravity of Things*, August 2017.

The afterword was written for *Boneshaker: A Bicycling Almanac* for the 2016 Lit Crawl PDX event in Portland, Oregon. RIP, Kenny.

Acknowledgments

Thanks to Leland Cheuk, who showed up to our Berkeley Hills writing group wearing the coolest, most don't-give-a-shit-about-feedback glasses. Here we are a decade-plus later. Gigi Little, for her book design and good humor. Lew Watts, for the cover image of me in 1989. Lori Hettler, for her hard work and enthusiasm. Heather Maxwell Hall, for her vision and generosity.

Much love to my family, especially my mom and dad, Chris Behr, Martha Noone, Sandy Walcott, and Tom Behr. Yin Ling Wong. Chas Nielsen. Margaret Murray. MFA sex biscuits: Amber Beaman, Danielle Vermette, Haili Jones Graff, and Sandra Stringer. Dardi Troen and Lincoln Miller. Christen and Scott Derr. Laura Stanfill. Support when I'm falling: Jennifer Stady, Jordan Foster, Sarah Berry, Deb Stone, and Kathleen Lane. Annie Herron and Jimmy Herron Zamora (RIP). Cynthia Gerdes, for your focus on the body during piano lessons.

Paul Cohen, Charlie D'Ambrosio, Craig Lesley, Michael McGregor, Tom Bissell, Whitney Otto, Karen Karbo, Emily Chenoweth, Matthew Dickman, and David Ciminello. Dan DeWeese and *Propeller.* Mary Rechner, Writers in the Schools, and all the brave teens. Evan P. Schneider and *Boneshaker.* Carrie Seitzinger and *Nailed.* Lidia Yuknavitch (bodies). Lee Montgomery (possibilities). Producers of *Mortified.* Meg Lemke and *Mutha.* Angela Patel, Jen Pastiloff, and *The Manifest-Station.* Jenny Forrester (Unchaste) and Michelle Fredette (Plonk). Fiona Bruce ("White Pants") and Scott Simmons ("Cuckoo"). Sally Shore, Holger Moncada, Jr., and Buckley Sampson for inhabiting my stories in Northern Writes. Residency at Sou'wester Lodge. Song titles from the Buzzcocks, Flipper, Iggy Pop, Nina Simone, and Sonic Youth.

Thanks forever to bandmates in The Double U, Born in a Car, Barbara Manning's Birthday Suit, Cindy Dall (RIP), Heavenly Ten Stems, Job's Daughters, Caroliner, Purple Oblivion, and Dumbhead.

Belief in the underground. Albus the cat. How you manifest your species.

Matt, for twenty-six years of a shared life. I saw your ghosts. And Eli Zheng, my soul love.

About the Author

Alex Behr has taught creative writing residencies at Portland, OR, high schools through Literary Arts' Writers in the Schools program. Alex's work has been published, or is forthcoming, in *Tin House*, *Salon*, *Nailed*, *Mutha*, *Bitch*, *Manifest-Station*, and other publications. She has performed nationwide in the comedy show *Mortified*. She can be found online at alexbehr.com and on Twitter @alex_behr.

7.13
BOOKS

CPSIA information can be obtained
at www.ICGtesting.com
Printed in the USA
FSOW02n1221251117
41346FS